'We're just your average, run-of-the-mill GPs' surgery, and I find it very hard to understand why Harry would offer to work here. So you tell me what's in it for Harry?'

'The pleasure of your company?'

Grace spun round when a familiar voice cut into the conversation. She spotted Harry lounging in the doorway. It had been some time since she'd seen him, but he'd changed very little from what she could tell. As her eyes skimmed over the coal-black hair, the marine-blue eyes, the clean-cut jaw, she couldn't stop the appreciative flutter her nerves gave—a warning that she was as susceptible as any woman to Harry Shaw's undoubted charms.

Jennifer Taylor lives in the north-west of England with her husband Bill. She had been writing Mills & Boon® romances for some years, but when she discovered Medical Romances™, she was so captivated by these heart-warming stories that she set out to write them herself! When she's not writing, or doing research for her latest book, Jennifer's hobbies include reading, travel, walking her dog and retail therapy (shopping!). Jennifer claims all that bending and stretching to reach the shelves is the best exercise possible. She's always delighted to hear from readers, so do visit her at www.jennifer-taylor.com

Recent titles by the same author:

A NIGHT TO REMEMBER
A BABY OF HIS OWN*
THE CONSULTANT'S ADOPTED SON*
IN HIS LOVING CARE*

*Bachelor Dads

THE WOMAN HE'S BEEN WAITING FOR

BY
JENNIFER TAYLOR

MILLS & BOON®

First published in Great Britain 2006
Paperback edition 2007
Harlequin Mills & Boon Limited,
Eton House, 18-24 Paradise Road, Richmond, Surrey TW9 1SR

© Jennifer Taylor 2006

ISBN-13: 978 0 263 85214 1
ISBN-10:   0 263 85214 8

Set in Times Roman 10½ on 12 pt
03-0107-53664

Printed and bound in Spain
by Litografia Rosés, S.A., Barcelona

THE WOMAN
HE'S BEEN
WAITING FOR

CHAPTER ONE

'WHAT do you mean *Harry Shaw* has offered to work here?'

Dr Grace Kennedy couldn't conceal her astonishment as she rounded on her partner, Miles Farrington. It was the end of a particularly stressful week at Ferndale Surgery and she and Miles had been trying to come up with a solution to their latest crisis when he had dropped his bombshell. Not only had their locum upped and left on New Year's Eve without giving them notice but yesterday their practice nurse had tripped and broken her ankle.

It would be some while before Alison was fit to return to work. In the meantime, they would have to manage without a nurse because they would never be able to find a replacement at this time of the year. There were a lot of reasons, in fact, why Grace was in no mood to play silly games.

'The same Harry Shaw who once said that only people without ambition went into general practice? Oh, this has to be a joke, Miles, please.'

'I don't recall Harry saying that about general practice...' Miles broke off when Grace glared at him. 'Harry was probably winding you up. You know what he's like. Anyway, he phoned me last night to say that he was in the area so I invited him round for a drink and just happened to mention the problems we were having during the course of the conversation. I was as surprised as you are when he offered his services, but you have to admit it would be the ideal solution. Oh, I know that you and Harry didn't exactly hit it off at med school—'

'And whose fault was that?' Grace paced across the room then swung round and scowled at her partner. 'Harry Shaw was a complete waste of space, in my opinion. The only thing he was interested in was seeing how many women he could sweet-talk into his bed.'

'Mmm, he did have rather an effect on the ladies,' Miles observed admiringly. He cleared his throat when he saw Grace's expression darken. 'But, all that aside, you have to admit that Harry was one of the brightest students in our year. It was the same during our pre-reg training when we were at Leeds together. It was Harry who was tipped for great things and he's achieved them, too. You must have followed his progress over the years, surely?'

Grace ignored the question. She had no intention of admitting that she'd been keeping tabs on Harry. To be frank, she wasn't sure why she'd bothered when she disliked the wretched man so much. Maybe it had been a way to prove to herself that she didn't care about professional glory and only wanted to do her job to the very best of her ability, but she could have recited Harry's CV from memory: the youngest consultant ever appointed to a post; Fellow of the Royal College of Physicians; member of the new government health service advisory committee…

'Then why does he want to work here?' Grace blanked out the rest of Harry's glittering résumé because it really wasn't relevant. She fixed Miles with a look that made him squirm but she refused to feel guilty. Once Miles got an idea into his head, it was difficult to make him see sense, but there was no way that she was going to agree to his latest proposal.

'Just look at the facts, Miles. We run a very busy rural practice here. We don't take private patients and we certainly don't have any VIPs on our list. We're just your average, run-of-the-mill GPs' surgery and I find it hard to understand why Harry would offer to work here. So you tell me, what's in it for Harry?'

'The pleasure of your company?'

Grace spun round when a familiar voice cut into the conversation. Her mouth thinned when she spotted Harry lounging in the doorway. It had been some time since she'd seen him but he'd changed very little from what she could tell. As her eyes skimmed over the coal-black hair, the marine-blue eyes, the clean-cut jaw, she couldn't stop the appreciative flutter her nerves gave, a warning that she was as susceptible as any woman to Harry Shaw's undoubted charms. The difference was that she knew what he was really like and she wasn't about to be taken in by good looks and a nice line in chat.

'I'm flattered, Harry. Or I would be if I was fool enough to believe you.' She treated him to a chilly smile which wavered when she saw the expression that crossed his face. Good heavens, surely Harry's feelings hadn't been hurt by that remark.

'Harry, good to see you again. I was beginning to wonder if you'd got lost. I'm hopeless at giving people directions, I'm afraid.' Miles leapt to his feet and rushed across the room to greet him.

Grace dismissed that fanciful notion when she realised what her partner had said. She looked accusingly at him as he led Harry over to the desk. 'You never mentioned that you'd invited Harry here tonight.'

'Didn't I? Purely an oversight, I assure you.' Miles fussed around, fetching a chair and taking Harry's overcoat. He hung it on the peg behind the door then looked pleadingly at Grace. 'I know we haven't had time to discuss this, but you know as well as I do that we desperately need help. I've been onto the agency every single day this week about hiring another locum but they simply haven't got anyone on their books willing to relocate at this time of the year. Nobody wants to spend the winter months in such a remote part of the country, apparently.'

'So what you're saying is that it's Harry or nothing,' Grace said sweetly.

'Well, I wouldn't put it quite like that,' Miles blustered in embarrassment, although Harry didn't seem the least perturbed by her bluntness.

'Why not, if it's true?' He clapped Miles on the shoulder then smiled at Grace. 'A bit of a dilemma for you, isn't it? It's a choice between letting me loose on your patients or going under. I'd find it very difficult to choose in your shoes, too, Gracie.'

'Don't call me that.' She sat down behind her desk and glared at him. 'You know how I hate stupid nicknames.'

'Sorry.'

He didn't sound sorry but short of making a fuss and thereby letting him think he'd scored a point, there was nothing she could do about it. She smiled up at him, her grey eyes colder than the January sky outside the consulting-room window. 'Apology accepted. So shall we start from the beginning? Why have you offered to work here when you made it abundantly clear in the past what you thought about general practice?'

'Because you and Miles need a helping hand.'

Harry sat down and crossed one long leg over the other as he waited for her next sally. Grace wasn't fool enough to go rushing in unprepared, however. She took the time to study him instead.

He was as impeccably dressed as ever, she noted sourly,

the black suit he was wearing obviously not something he'd picked up off the peg. He'd teamed it with a pale blue shirt and a jaunty red and blue silk tie that must have cost a small fortune, but, then, money had never been a problem for Harry because his family was loaded. Harry was used to having the best of everything and it showed.

By contrast, poor Miles looked even more dishevelled than usual. Miles had been struggling to cope since his wife, Penny, had found out last month that she was pregnant. Penny had lost a baby only the previous year and they were both desperate that she didn't lose this one, so Miles had insisted that Penny must do as little as possible during the first trimester. However, it had put him under even more pressure and it was starting to show.

Grace knew that Miles had been doing far too much, but there was little she could do to help when her own workload seemed to be increasing on an almost daily basis. The truth was that the practice was getting far too big for the two of them to manage. Maybe it wouldn't be *that* bad, having Harry here, if it gave them a respite, she conceded grudgingly.

'How about a cup of coffee?' Miles suggested, jumping up. He rubbed his chest and grimaced. 'That'll teach me to bolt my lunch. I've had indigestion all afternoon. I'd better take some antacids while I'm at it.'

'Don't go to any trouble on my account,' Harry said easily. 'I'll be having dinner when I get back to the hotel.'

'Oh, it's no trouble. Anyway, it will give you and Grace a chance to talk and see if you can reach a compromise.' Miles turned to her and Grace could see the beseeching look in his eyes. 'Just don't say no before you've had time to think about the idea.'

Grace didn't say anything. She didn't want to upset Miles but neither was she prepared to be pushed into a decision she might come to regret. She waited until the door had closed before she turned to Harry again.

'All right, I'm willing to admit that having you here would be a big help at the moment, but how come you happen to have so much free time on your hands? The last I heard you'd been appointed to some new government health committee. I'd have thought you would have had enough to do with that on top of your job at St Theresa's.'

'St Theresa's has been undergoing a major refurbishment programme for the past two years. Obviously, we couldn't close the whole hospital while the work was being done so we've had to shut each department in turn.' He shrugged. 'It's our turn at the moment, so it seemed like the ideal opportunity to take some of the time I had owing to me.'

'It won't be much of a holiday if you end up working here,' she pointed out.

'Oh, I don't know. They say that a change is as good as a rest, don't they?' he quipped, tipping back his chair and grinning at her.

It was the sort of smile that Grace had seen him bestow dozens of times before on some poor unsuspecting woman or other, but if Harry thought he could turn on the charm and get her to agree to his proposal, he was mistaken. Harry never did anything unless it furthered his own interests and she wasn't about to let him fob her off with any nonsense.

'I can't see any point in trying to have a sensible discussion if that's your attitude.' She went to stand up then stopped when Harry leant across the desk. Her heart jolted when she saw how serious he looked. Normally, Harry treated life as a huge joke just there for his enjoyment and it was unsettling to see this other side of him for once.

'I'm sorry. I know how you feel about me, Grace. I should do because you've always made it perfectly clear that you doubted my motives. So to answer your question properly, I happened to be in the area on business rather than on holiday. Working here for a couple of weeks won't spoil my plans one little bit.'

He didn't explain what sort of business had brought him all the way to Cumbria and Grace didn't ask. What Harry did was of little interest to her, except where it impinged on her own life, of course.

'I see. Now that your business has been concluded, you have some free time on your hands.' Her brows rose steeply when he nodded. 'That's very altruistic of you, Harry. Not many people would offer to give up their time off like this.'

'I just want to help. Miles told me about your locum leaving and what had happened to your practice nurse. You might feel that you can cope, Grace, but Miles obviously doesn't share your confidence. Quite frankly, he sounded as though he'd reached the end of his tether last night. It's obvious the two of you are under a tremendous amount of pressure and I think you need to take that into account before you turn me down.'

'I don't need you to remind me about the pressure we're under,' she snapped, because Harry had touched a nerve. Although she and Miles shared the responsibility of running the practice, she couldn't ignore the fact that Miles had the added worry of Penny to contend with. Not for the first time Grace found herself thinking how fortunate she was not to have to worry about anyone else. She was single out of choice and happy with her life.

Or she was most of the time.

She wasn't sure where that qualification had sprung from and quickly dismissed it. Thoughts like that would only clutter up her mind and that could prove disastrous when dealing with Harry. She sat down again and treated him to a look that was meant to prove she was in control of the situation. The problem was that Harry looked so worried that she couldn't help feeling alarmed, too.

'I'm not trying to start an argument with you, Grace. It might surprise you to learn that I didn't come here tonight for a fight. I came because I was worried about Miles. Have you looked at him recently?'

'Of course I have. I see him nearly every day of the week. What kind of a stupid question is that?'

'I mean *really* looked at him.' Harry sat back in his chair and regarded her thoughtfully. His blue eyes were so intent that Grace found it impossible to look away.

'I didn't realise there were different ways of looking at people,' she snapped, because he was making her feel really uncomfortable now.

She tucked a loose strand of hair behind her ear then realised what she was doing. She wasn't going to start worrying about how she looked because of Harry. No way, not in a million years. So what if she was wearing her oldest sweater—the one with the worn patches on the elbows—and a skirt that should have been sent to the charity shop months ago? And what did it matter if her nose was shiny and her hair needed brushing? She'd worked non-stop from the moment she'd arrived that morning and she'd been far too busy to worry about her appearance. Maybe Harry had the time to choose the perfect tie to go with his perfect shirt and perfect suit, but lesser mortals didn't.

She opened her mouth to tell Harry that only he'd carried on speaking. Grace felt a tremor work its way from the tips of her toes to her knees when she heard what he was saying. She wanted to stop him but some perverse little imp inside her refused to coperate.

'There's dozens of ways of looking at people. It just depends who they are and what they mean to you. It also makes a difference how long it's been since you saw them, too.' Harry made a steeple with his fingers and studied her over the top of the spire. 'Take you, for instance, Grace. It must be almost a year since we last saw each other and you look very different now from what you did then. Your hair is shorter for starters and although it suits you, I have to say that I think it's a shame you've had it cut because that caramel-brown colour is so unusual. You've also lost weight. Not a lot, granted, but you're definitely slimmer.'

'Thank you, Harry. I think you've made your point now.'

Grace brusquely cut him off. She couldn't explain it, but the fact that Harry had noticed the changes in her appearance made her feel very odd indeed. It was as though he was seeing her as a woman for the first time and she couldn't pretend that it didn't make her feel extremely conscious of her own femininity all of a sudden.

'Then you understand what I'm getting at, don't you?' Mercifully, Harry seemed unaware of her dilemma as he continued. 'You see Miles every day so you probably haven't noticed the change in him, but I was shocked when I saw him last night. To be honest, I almost didn't recognise him at first. He looks like he's aged five years in the past twelve months.'

'It's been tough for Miles this past year,' Grace conceded. She sighed when Harry's brows rose. She could hardly refuse to explain that comment. Anyway, it might divert his interest away from her and that would be a blessing.

'I don't suppose I'm betraying any confidences because Miles has never made any secret of the fact that he and Penny have been having problems,' she said quickly, not sure why she was so sensitive all of a sudden. She and Harry had traded enough insults to sink a fleet of battleships over the years and she couldn't imagine why she should have been so alarmed by his comments.

'*Problems.* You don't mean with their marriage, do you?'

Harry sounded so shocked by the suggestion that she looked at him in surprise. 'Of course not. Their marriage is rock solid and they're really happy together. Everything would be perfect, in fact, if they could just have the family they're both longing for, but Penny's had problems conceiving. She had a miscarriage last year so now that she's pregnant again, Miles is taking no chances. He's insisted that she must rest as much as possible, but that means he's been trying to do everything himself.'

'Not easy when you're so busy here,' Harry agreed soberly. He sighed, his handsome face looking unaccustomedly sad. 'It's such a shame. Miles and Penny are the kind of people who make you want to believe in all that happily-ever-after nonsense. So many marriages fail that it's nice to see a couple actually making a go of it.'

'I never thought you'd be an advocate for marriage,' Grace observed tartly, to hide her surprise. She'd never expected to hear Harry expounding on the joys of matrimony. It simply didn't go with the image she had of him and it was unsettling to think that she might have to adjust her ideas.

'Oh, I'm a great believer in the institution of marriage,' he declared. 'So long as I don't have to get personally involved in promoting it as a lifestyle choice then I'm more than happy to give it my vote.'

'Typical,' Grace snorted. 'Why would you want to spoil your fun by making a commitment to one woman when you can have your pick from dozens? I'm just surprised you found the time to come here tonight, Harry, when you could be using it so much more productively.'

'Oh, the night is young yet and there's plenty of time left for…pleasure.'

His deep voice lingered on the last word and the tiny hairs on the back of Grace's neck sprang to attention. She had a sudden and far too vivid mental picture of how Harry might pleasure the latest woman in his life, so she quickly stood up. Harry might be prepared to sit here and play these silly games but she wasn't going to play them with him.

'How very nice for you. Now, if you'll excuse me, I'd like to have a word with Miles before I make my decision.'

'Of course. But take your time, Grace, and really think about what you're doing. I'd hate you to turn down my offer and then regret it.'

Harry stood up as she came round the desk and she was forced to stop. He was several inches taller than she was so that she had to tip back her head to look at him. Maybe it was that which made her feel so vulnerable all of a sudden.

'I want you to be sure in your own heart, Grace, that you really don't want me here.'

Harry knew he shouldn't tease Grace like that but it was hard to resist when she always rose so sweetly to his baiting. He hid his smile as he watched a dozen different expressions cross her face. She was trying to decide whether she should ignore him or tear a strip off him, and he realised with a sudden flash of insight that he didn't mind which it was. Fighting with Grace was a whole lot more fun than making love had been with many of the women he'd dated over the past few years.

The thought caught him unawares so it was a relief when Grace swept past him without uttering a word. Harry went to the window after she'd left, wondering where the idea had sprung from. Grace Kennedy had been a pain in the butt ever since he'd met her on their first day at Oxford together. She'd taken an instant dislike to him and had never once missed the opportunity to goad him since then.

Harry had found himself responding in kind even though he'd known he should try to rise above such childish behaviour. It was just that Grace's remarks had seemed to prick harder and more painfully than anyone else's had done. She'd been one of the top students in their year so he'd told himself that it was competitiveness that had caused the problem: Grace had resented the fact that he was every bit as talented as she was and that was why she'd given him hell, and it had become a point of honour that he should retaliate. Now he found himself wondering if there was another reason why they'd kept up the sparring for all these years. Was it possible that he and Grace were attracted to each other?

He groaned. It was obviously a night for stupid thoughts. He didn't seriously imagine that Grace found him attractive. They argued because she neither liked nor trusted him, and because he refused to do anything to improve her opinion of him. It made him see how difficult it would be for them to work together in such circumstances. It wouldn't help poor Miles if he and Grace were constantly at odds.

He sighed as he stared across the empty car park. It was a blow to face that fact, when he'd thought that he'd found the ideal solution to his problems as well as Miles's. He'd never got around to telling Miles last night the reason why he was in Cumbria. Miles had been so stressed that he hadn't found the right moment to broach the subject, which was ironic, really, because this new health service committee he'd been appointed to had been set up specifically to find ways to relieve the pressure on rural GPs.

Harry had spoken to dozens of general practitioners over the past few weeks, but he still hadn't been able to get a true picture of all the problems they faced. Few people liked to admit they couldn't cope and GPs were no different to anyone else in that respect. He'd been hoping to get some truthful answers out of Miles, but once he'd learned about the difficulties his friend was experiencing, Harry had realised it was the opportunity he needed. If he offered to work at the surgery then not only would he be helping Miles but he'd be able to experience the pressures at first hand.

He'd decided to talk to Miles and Grace about it that evening, but now he could see how pointless it would be. Although he was confident that Miles would agree to his proposal, Grace certainly wouldn't. She'd probably see it as a slight on the way they ran the practice and the last thing Harry wanted was to create a rift between the two partners. All things considered, it might be better if he told Miles that he'd changed his mind.

'Can you phone for an ambulance?'

Grace came rushing back into the room. Harry felt his heart sink when he saw the expression on her face. 'What's wrong?' he demanded as he watched her wrench open a cupboard door.

'It's Miles. I th-think h-he's having a heart attack.'

Her voice caught and she bit her lip. Harry could see that her hands were shaking as she tried to take a syringe out of the box. He hurried across the room and took it from her then looked around.

'Drugs?'

'In that steel cabinet in the corner. Here's the keys.'

She handed him a bunch of keys. Harry took them and quickly unlocked the cupboard. 'You phone for an ambulance while I sort this out,' he instructed, checking through the vials until he found what he needed.

'Oh, but—'

'For heavens sake, Grace, don't waste time arguing. Just do it.'

He didn't wait to see how she took that: there wasn't

time. He left her in the office and ran along the corridor, cursing under his breath because he'd forgotten to ask her where he would find Miles. Fortunately, there were only three other doors leading off the corridor and he found Miles propped up against the sink unit in the staffroom.

'How's it going, old man?' Harry asked, dropping to his knees beside him.

'I've had better days,' Miles muttered, clutching his chest.

'I'll bet you have.' Harry quickly rolled up his friend's shirtsleeve and swabbed his arm then slid the needle into his vein. 'There. That should ease the pain in a moment or two so let's take a look at you.'

He took hold of Miles's wrist and checked his pulse. It was a little fast but strong enough, and he smiled encouragingly at him. 'Well, the old ticker's still working away, you'll be pleased to hear.'

'Nice to know I'm not dead yet,' Miles replied with a brave stab at humour.

'Oh, there's plenty of life in the old dog yet,' Harry said airily, hoping he wasn't tempting fate.

He carried on with his examination, looking for all the usual signs he would expect to find in a case of myocardial infarction, things like shortness of breath, sweating and an absence of colour in the skin. Miles was exhibiting all of those symptoms, worryingly enough, so Harry was relieved when Grace appeared to tell him the ambulance was on its way.

'Good. Hospital's the best place for you,' he declared as Grace knelt down beside them. She lent forward to loosen the collar of Miles's shirt and Harry sucked in his breath when he felt a stab of awareness hit him squarely in the gut as her shoulder brushed against his chest.

He hastily stood up. The last thing he needed was for his mind to start playing those tricks again. He didn't fancy Grace any more than she fancied him. The pattern of their relationship had been set years ago and this definitely wasn't the time to start altering it. He adopted a deliberately neutral expression when she glanced up because he didn't intend to make the mistake of handing her any ammunition to use against him in the future.

'The ambulance should be here soon but I'm worried they might not be able to find us,' she explained anxiously. 'It's really dark at this end of the village and I'd hate them to miss the turning and drive straight past.'

'I'll go and wait by the gates so I can flag them down,' Harry offered, relieved to have something to do. 'You stay here and look after Miles.'

'Thanks, Harry. That would be a real help. I appreciate it.'

It was the first time Harry could remember her ever speaking to him with any warmth in her voice. As he left the kitchen, he found himself marvelling at the effect it'd had. He wanted to leap up and punch the air as though he'd scored a major victory, although he had no idea why. Grace had merely treated him on a par with everyone else. She'd spoken to him as a normal human being instead of as her worst enemy. Why that should be a cause for celebration, he couldn't imagine.

He left the surgery and headed down the drive. It was a bitterly cold night and his overcoat was still hanging on the back of the consulting-room door, but he never noticed the discomfort. His head seemed to be whirling, thoughts spinning around inside it like the bits of coloured glass whizzing about inside that kaleidoscope he'd had as a kid. One thought suddenly caught and took shape.

Sparring with Grace had been a lot of fun, but what would it be like if they could talk to each other and discover all the things they had in common?

The idea dissolved before he could attempt to deal with it and another took its place.

And if they did achieve a degree of harmony, then wouldn't it be a shame to stop there? After all, Grace was a beautiful woman and he'd never denied that, so wouldn't it be great if they could establish a more intimate relationship…

The wail of a siren came as a blessing in more ways than one. As he flagged down the ambulance, Harry felt like a condemned man must feel on receiving a last-minute pardon. He had no idea what was prompting all these crazy thoughts but one thing was certain: he and Grace would never have that kind of a relationship.

CHAPTER TWO

'WHY doesn't someone come and tell us what's happening?'

'These things take time, Penny, so try not to worry. They'll let us know how Miles is just as soon as they can.'

Grace put a comforting arm around Penny's shoulders but the long wait was taking its toll on her, too. She glanced at her watch and sighed when she realised that over an hour had passed since Miles had been admitted to the emergency department of their local hospital. She'd travelled in the ambulance with him while Harry had gone to fetch Penny. He'd seemed to take it for granted that he would stay with them, and Grace had to admit that she'd been glad of his support. Harry seemed to have the knack of knowing the right thing to say to calm Penny down so now she glanced at him and raised her brows.

'Grace is right, sweetheart. You must try not to worry.' Harry obviously took the hint because he got up and came over to them. 'You know how long it takes to get a heart tracing and do all the bloods and everything else.'

'I know, and I'm sorry, but it's just so hard to sit here when I don't even know if Miles… If he's…he's….' Penny stopped and gulped, unable to give voice to her very worst fears.

'If anything awful had happened to Miles, they'd have come and told you.' Harry crouched down and took hold of Penny's hands. 'You remember the drill, don't you? You should do because you were an A and E nurse for long enough. You inform the relatives immediately if it's bad news. It's one of the unwritten rules.'

'I remember,' Penny whispered, dredging up a smile. 'It's just so different when you're the one waiting to hear something.'

'I know, sweetheart, but you must try to be strong for Miles and for your baby.'

He leant forward and kissed Penny's cheek. Grace felt a lump come to her throat. This wasn't Harry Shaw using his legendary charm to his own ends but a bona fide show of concern, and there was no denying that it had touched her deeply to witness it.

'I'll try. Thank you, Harry. And you, too, Grace.' Penny took hold of Grace's hand and placed it on top of Harry's. 'You two are the best. I don't know what I'd have done without you both tonight.'

Grace's heartbeat quickened when she felt the warmth of Harry's hand beneath her palm. She desperately wanted to pull away but she didn't want to risk upsetting Penny. She sat quite still, praying that Harry couldn't feel how fast her pulse was racing. This is just a moment of friendship, she told herself firmly. Penny needs it to help her through this difficult time. However, it was hard to focus on that thought when she was so conscious of the warmth of Harry's flesh beneath her own. It was a relief when a nurse appeared because it meant that she could quite legitimately break the contact.

'Mrs Farrington?' The nurse smiled as Penny hastily identified herself. 'You can see your husband now.'

'Is he all right?' Penny demanded, jumping to her feet.

'He's fine. Dr Williams will explain everything if you'll just follow me.'

'Yes, of course.' Penny hurried to the door then paused and looked back. 'Will you stay? I know it's late but I don't think I can face being here on my own.'

'We'll be right here, waiting for you, Penny,' Grace assured her. She let out a sigh of relief after the door closed. 'Doesn't sound as though the prognosis is too grim. Do you think Miles really did have an infarc?'

'It's hard to say for certain without seeing the ECG tracings,' Harry replied, going over to the coffee-machine. 'It could have been an angina attack, I suppose. The symptoms are very similar.'

'Mmm, you could be right.' Grace frowned as she considered that possibility. 'Miles is rather young to be suffering from angina, although it's not unknown. Most patients are in their fifties when they first exhibit any symptoms but there are cases of men as young as thirty being diagnosed with angina.'

'It's not just confined to men either. More and more women are presenting with angina nowadays,' Harry observed, feeding coins into the machine.

'That's true. Women are having more heart attacks than they used to. It's all down to a change in lifestyle and the fact that people are eating more convenience food and not taking enough exercise.' She sighed. 'I try to drum it into our patients that they need to exercise and watch their diet, but they just think I'm nagging.'

'Until they have a heart attack and realise that you were telling them the truth all along.' Harry handed her a cup of tepid coffee and sat down. 'Then they're desperate to undo all the years of neglect.'

'Something like that,' she agreed, sipping the coffee and grimacing at the powdery aftertaste it left on her tongue. She put the cup on the table and looked at him. 'How come you're so clued up about heart disease?'

'Because it's all part and parcel of being a physician.' Harry took a swallow of his coffee then sighed. 'If I had a pound for every man and woman I've seen heading for a heart attack, I'd be able to retire. What is it about people that makes them ignore all the advice we give them and carry on doing the wrong things?'

'Stubbornness?' she suggested with a grin because he sounded so frustrated. 'Folk hate to be told what to do. They want to live their lives the way they chose to.'

'And to hell with the consequences.' His tone was wry. 'Only, when something does go wrong, they expect us to come up with a solution.'

'I don't know why you sound so surprised. Didn't you realise that we're supposed to perform miracles? It's part of our remit, along with all the other things a doctor is supposed to do.'

'Well, I for one am right out of miracles,' Harry declared, swinging his feet onto the coffee-table. 'I'm only a humble physician, don't forget, not a surgeon. It's the surgeons who are closest to God, not the likes of you and me.'

Grace burst out laughing. 'I never thought I'd hear you admit that. I thought you believed that you had a direct line to heaven.'

'Sorry to disappoint you but I'm under no illusions.' He lifted the cup to his lips, watching her over the rim. 'I'm just a guy who wants to help people, Grace. That's all I've ever been.'

Grace felt a shiver run down her spine and quickly looked away. She couldn't explain it, but there was something about the way Harry had said it that convinced her he'd been telling the truth. Harry didn't see himself as some sort of all-powerful being but as a man who wanted to help others less fortunate than himself, and it was a revelation to realise it.

She'd had Harry summed up from the moment she'd met him: a rich playboy whose only aim in life was to have a good time and cover himself in glory. Now that image had started to go all fuzzy around the edges and it was alarming to realise that she might have been wrong about him all this time. It was a relief when he changed the subject.

'Anyway, getting back to Miles. Even if he hasn't had an infarc, it's doubtful he'll be fit enough to return to work for some time, so what are you going to do? My offer still stands, if you're interested.'

'I'll bear it in mind.' Grace flushed when his brows rose. It was obvious that her less-than-enthusiastic response hadn't been lost on him. However, she didn't intend to apologise because she had reservations about him working at the surgery.

'I'd prefer to wait and see what the verdict is on Miles first before I decide what to do,' she told him coolly.

'Fine. It's up to you, of course.' Harry drained his cup then swung his feet off the table and stood up. 'I think I'll go outside for a bit of fresh air. It's stifling in here. I won't be long—ten minutes max.'

'You don't have to stay,' she said quickly, hoping he couldn't tell how eager she was all of a sudden for him to leave. Oh, it had been fine while Penny had been there, she'd been very glad of Harry's company then. However, it was different now they were on their own. In the past half-hour she'd learned things about him that she'd never dreamed might be true, and it had unsettled her to have to adjust her view of him. How much more unsettling would it be if they continued the conversation throughout the night?

'Why do I have a feeling that you're trying to get rid of me?' Harry turned to look at her and Grace's heart missed a beat when she saw the speculation in his eyes.

'I've no idea.' She shrugged, hoping he couldn't tell

how desperate she was for him to leave. 'Maybe it's because you find it hard to believe that I'll be able to manage without your manly shoulder to lean on? Well, don't worry, Harry. I'll be perfectly fine on my own so you can leave with a clear conscience. I'm sure you must have more interesting things to do with your evening than spend it hanging around a hospital waiting room.'

'The only plans I have for this evening involve bed.' He laughed when he saw her mouth purse. 'Tut, tut, Grace, what *are* you thinking? I meant that I was planning on having an early night—alone.' He opened the door and winked at her. 'Don't worry, I'll be back soon. You can count on it.'

Grace ground her teeth, wishing that she'd never said anything. All she'd succeeded in doing had been to make herself look foolish—not that it was the first time, of course. Where Harry was concerned she invariably found herself saying the wrong thing, which was why she usually resorted to squabbling with him. It was easier to fight with him than run the risk of falling under his spell.

The thought alarmed her so much that she leapt to her feet. Her heart was pounding as she left the waiting room to go and find Penny because there was no way that she could deny the truth. In the past ten years she'd done everything in her power to shut Harry out of her life. That was why she'd lobbed insults at him, goaded him and accused him of all manner of things. She'd seen how charming he could be, how witty and how much fun, and she'd been afraid that he would somehow…well, seduce her.

That was the last thing she wanted to happen. She'd witnessed at first hand how destructive love could be, had watched as her mother's life had been torn apart as her father had indulged in one affair after another, and she'd sworn it would never happen to her. That's why she rarely dated and never went out with any man who reminded her of her father—a man exactly like Harry, in fact. But tonight she'd lowered her guard and Harry had been every bit as charming as she'd feared he would be. Now she was unable to think of him simply as a womanising Lothario. There were depths to Harry that she'd never suspected.

'I get off at eleven so why don't you give me a call? I'm a real night-owl and never go to bed until after midnight…unless I have a really good reason, of course.'

Grace stopped dead when she heard voices up ahead. She peered along the dimly lit corridor and spotted a couple tucked into the alcove next to the pay-phone. She recognised Harry immediately, although it took a moment longer before she realised that the young woman with him was the nurse who'd come to fetch Penny. There were no prizes for guessing what they were up to, however.

Grace's eyes narrowed as she studied their body language which, quite frankly, should have been X-rated. The way that young nurse was simpering up at Harry was positively obscene. As for Harry—well, he seemed to be lapping it up as though it was his due. Had he used the excuse that he'd needed some fresh air so he could track down the nurse and make his move on her? Grace wondered in disgust. Well, if that was the case, she certainly wasn't going to cramp his style.

She spun round and marched back to the waiting room, slamming the door behind her with enough force to make the window rattle in its frame. She couldn't believe what a fool she'd been. For a few minutes she'd actually believed that she'd been wrong about Harry, and the thought of how easily he had duped her made her want to spit tacks. Leopards *never* changed their spots. Harry Shaw had been a womanising Lothario when she'd first met him, and he was exactly the same now.

* * *

'I'm not really sure what's happening tonight.'

Harry tried to edge away but the nurse had effectively trapped him in the alcove. He glanced along the corridor when he heard a door slam, hoping that someone would come along and rescue him. However, his hopes were dashed when nobody appeared. He sighed under his breath. He would just have to extricate himself.

'I'll probably end up staying here until all hours of the morning and I couldn't possibly expect you to wait up for my call.'

He treated the girl to his most charming smile, desperately wishing that he didn't have this effect on women. Although it sounded arrogant to say so, it had always been the same—they fell for his looks and the fact that he was wealthy. While it had been fun when he had been younger, he'd grown weary of being viewed merely as an object of their lust.

He wanted a proper relationship now, not the kind of shallow alliance that was based solely on sex. He wanted a relationship in which he could share his innermost thoughts and feelings. The kind of rapport, in fact, that he'd enjoyed tonight with Grace before she'd gone all prickly on him again.

The thought caught him completely off guard. Harry found himself floundering when the nurse asked if he had a pen so she could write down her telephone number for him. He gave it to her then waited in silence while she scribbled the number on a bit of paper and tucked it in his top pocket. Mercifully, the ward sister appeared at that point and summoned her back to work so he was able to make his escape, but he couldn't deny that he felt completely out of kilter as he made his way back to the waiting room.

Why did he keep having all these strange thoughts

about Grace? Was it just the fact that she'd treated him differently that night—talked to him, laughed with him, behaved as though he wasn't the lowest form of pond life? He wasn't convinced that was the reason why he was behaving so strangely, but he felt unusually nervous as he went into the room.

'Any news yet?' he asked, striving for a measure of calm.

'You tell me.' Grace treated him to a smile so cold that it could have reversed the effects of global warming, and Harry frowned.

'What's that supposed to mean?'

'Work it out for yourself. It shouldn't be that difficult for an intelligent man like you, Harry.'

She picked up a magazine and proceeded to ignore him as she flicked through its pages. Harry sighed because he really wasn't in the mood to play games with her at the moment.

'Look, Grace, I apologise if I've done something to upset you—' he began, but she didn't let him finish. Tossing the magazine onto the table, she glared at him.

'I am *not* upset. If you want to chat up every single woman in this hospital then good luck to you. However, I do object to being told a pack of lies. If you wanted to go and find that nurse, why didn't you say so? I'm hardly going to fall down in a heap because you're chatting up some woman.'

So that was it. Harry felt a wave of relief wash over him. Grace must have seen him talking to that nurse and assumed he'd engineered the meeting. He hastened to reassure her, even though he wasn't sure why it was so important that she knew what had really gone on.

'I did go out for some fresh air. I just happened to bump into Cathy on my way back, that's all.'

'Oh, so it's Cathy, is it? Obviously, you didn't waste any time getting acquainted with her.'

Grace treated him to another of those icy smiles and he sighed again. It was obvious that she didn't believe he was the innocent party.

'Just because I know her name doesn't mean that your allegations are true,' he pointed out in his most reasonable tone. 'It happened exactly as I told you. I was coming back inside when she stopped me.' He shrugged. 'I couldn't just ignore her, could I?'

'Of course not. I mean, it would have been unthinkable to tell her that you were far too worried about your friend to think about your…uh…*other* needs.'

Her voice dripped with scorn and Harry gritted his teeth. It took a massive effort of will to damp down his anger, but he really and truly didn't want to fight with her right now.

Was that what she was trying to do? he wondered. Poke and prod at him until he retaliated? He sensed it was true yet he couldn't understand why she would do such a thing. Unless she was afraid that if they didn't argue, she might be forced to admit that she was jealous of the attention he'd been paying the other woman.

The thought was so mind-bogglingly complicated that he didn't know how to handle it. He was still struggling, in fact, when the door opened and Penny appeared. Grace jumped up, ignoring him as she led Penny to a chair and sat her down.

'How is Miles?' she demanded, sitting beside her.

'Much better than I feared.' Penny gave them a wobbly smile. 'They're fairly sure that he suffered an angina attack rather than a full-blown myocardial infarction. The resting ECG tracing shows no sign of damage to his heart but they want to do more tests tomorrow—get Miles onto the treadmill to see how his heart responds during exercise. The consultant I spoke to seems fairly confident that it was a coronary artery spasm, though.'

'Probably brought on by the pressure that Miles has been under recently,' Harry observed, relieved to have something to focus on other than what Grace might or might not be thinking. 'Let's face it, Miles has been running himself ragged of late. It was just a matter of time before something like this happened.'

'I know, and that's why I'm determined that he's going to have a complete rest.' Penny took a deep breath then looked at him and Grace. 'I know you two have had your differences in the past, but if you could just put them aside for now, you could actually be saving Miles's life. He needs complete rest and the only way he'll get it is if he knows the practice is being taken care of. I know it's a lot to ask, but do you think you two could manage to work together for the next couple of weeks?'

CHAPTER THREE

HARRY knew that if Penny had asked him that question a couple of hours ago, he wouldn't have hesitated. He would have told her quite emphatically that there wouldn't be a problem. Now he was no longer sure if it was the truth. Could he really imagine himself working with Grace when just a few hours of her company had caused such an upheaval in his life?

'I...um...well...' he stumbled as his usual composure deserted him.

'I wouldn't ask if I wasn't desperate.' There were tears in Penny's eyes now as she looked up at him. 'I just can't bear to think of anything happening to Miles, especially now.'

She laid her hand protectively on her stomach and Harry knew he was sunk. How could he turn his back on his two oldest friends when they needed his help so desperately? He wouldn't be able to live with himself if anything happened to Miles or this precious baby, so he would have to agree and simply hope that he and Grace could get through the coming weeks relatively unscathed.

He turned to Grace, praying that she couldn't tell how uneasy he felt at the thought of their forthcoming alliance. 'I'm willing to give it a shot if you are.' He held out his hand. 'So, shall we call a truce?'

An expression which looked almost like panic crossed her face before she quickly stood up. 'All right. I'm willing to meet you halfway, if it means we're helping Miles and Penny.'

Harry smiled wryly. It hadn't been panic at all, but Grace being her usual cautious self. It was typical of her to qualify her agreement like that, to make sure he knew that she was accepting his offer purely for the sake of their friends. She would never admit to any sign of weakness in front of him, never acknowledge that she, too, would benefit from his help in the surgery. She would never give an inch if it meant he might gain any ground, and maybe it was that thought that made him decide to seal their agreement with more than the customary handshake. The thought of getting a little further under Grace's skin was oddly appealing.

He took her outstretched hand but instead of shaking it, as she'd expected him to do, he pulled her towards him and kissed her on the cheek. 'Sealed with a kiss. There's no going back on our pact now, Grace.'

He let her go, hoping she couldn't tell the effect the kiss had had on him. It was his own fault for trying to goad her, but it had been ages since he'd felt this stirring in his blood, so long, in fact, that he'd begun to wonder if it would ever happen again. Yet all it had taken had been the touch of his lips against her skin and he was all fired up and raring to go. What was happening to him? Did he fancy Grace, or was he going completely crazy?

'I wouldn't dream of going back on a promise,' Grace said stiffly. She turned to Penny, trying to resist the urge to run her hand over her cheek. She could feel the lingering warmth of Harry's lips making her skin tingle and longed to erase it, but there was no way that she was going to let him think that the kiss had had any effect on her.

'It looks as though your problem has been solved, Penny. Now there's no excuse for Miles not to follow his consultant's advice.'

'And I intend to make sure he follows it to the letter.' Penny stood up and hugged her. 'Thank you so much, Grace. And you, too, Harry. I can't tell you how grateful I am to you both.'

'Don't mention it.' Harry treated them to one of his most charming smiles, the kind of smile that normally made Grace grind her teeth. The fact that she didn't feel like grinding them now just increased her anxiety. What on earth was going on? Why did she feel all warm and sort of…breathless just because Harry was smiling at her? She was still trying to work out the answer when he opened the waiting-room door.

'I won't be long. There's something I need to do before we leave.'

'Hmm, that something wouldn't have anything to do with a pretty blonde nurse who's been extolling your virtues to all and sundry, would it?' Penny laughed when he looked suitably modest. 'You never change, Harry. You'll still have women queuing up outside your door when you're ninety.'

'With a bit of luck.'

He winked at them then left, and it was a good job he went when he did. Grace knew that if he'd stayed there even a second longer, she would have been tempted to throw something at him. Maybe Penny found his woman-ising antics amusing but she thought they were pathetic.

'Grace, what's wrong? Are you feeling all right?'

She jumped when Penny touched her on the arm, and dredged up a smile when she saw the concern on her friend's face. 'I'm fine.'

'Are you sure?' Penny looked increasingly worried

despite the reassurance. 'I shouldn't have done that, should I? I know how you feel about Harry and it was wrong of me to force you into a corner like that.'

'You didn't force me, Penny. It was my decision and I'm perfectly happy with it.' Grace held her smile, although it felt as though her face was about to split into two. However, she had to convince Penny that she was telling the truth, otherwise her friend would continue to worry.

'Harry and I are both grown-ups and we can handle working together without World War Three breaking out. In fact, I'm rather looking forward to it.'

'You are?' Penny looked at her in surprise.

'Mmm. Harry's got bags of experience and I'll learn a lot from him,' Grace assured her, hoping the words wouldn't choke her.

'Yes, of course you will, although it won't be all one-sided,' Penny said loyally. 'You're a brilliant doctor in your own right, Grace, so I expect Harry will learn just as much from you.'

Grace didn't say anything to that. However, as she followed Penny from the room so they could go and tell Miles the good news, she found herself wondering exactly what she had in her repertoire of skills which would be of interest to Harry. There certainly wasn't anything on the romance front that she could teach him—he was an acknowledged expert in that field. As for her medical skills, well, he could probably match her any day of the week.

No, the only thing she could possibly teach him was humility, although it was a lesson the mighty Harry Shaw might not be keen to learn. When you've been at the top of the heap all your life, thinking that you are the same as everyone else wouldn't come easily, although that wasn't what Harry had claimed earlier that night. He'd described himself as a man who just wanted to help others, hadn't he?

Grace shivered. She couldn't explain it, certainly couldn't understand it, but she knew the assertion had altered the way she thought about Harry. It was as though there was suddenly something in the plus column to weigh against all those minuses that had accumulated over the years. Although she hated to admit it, Harry might not be all bad after all.

'I've done a printout of all the clinics we hold each month. I thought it would help if you had an idea of our schedule.'

'Thanks.'

Harry took the list from Grace and glanced through it. His brows rose when he suddenly realised the extent of the work she and Miles had been doing. Nearly every single afternoon was filled with things like the mother-and-baby clinics, antenatal clinics and clinics for people who were trying to stop smoking or lose weight. Add all of those to the regular morning and evening surgeries and it seemed his life was going to be extremely full for the next few weeks.

'You certainly offer a very complete service here,' he observed, leaning back in his chair. It was just gone eight a.m. and they were in Miles's office—the office Harry would be using while he was working there. Although it had been after midnight when he'd dropped Grace off at her house in the village, she had telephoned him before seven that morning to ask him if he would meet her at the surgery.

Harry had agreed immediately, even though he'd been fast asleep when she'd phoned. However, it had seemed like a point of honour not to let the side down so he had dragged himself out of bed and into the shower, and, by skipping breakfast, had managed to get to the surgery a couple of minutes before she'd arrived. He could have murdered for a cup of coffee but he'd be damned if he would show any sign of weakness by suggesting they should stop for a drink. If Grace could keep up this punishing schedule then so could he.

'We do our best to fulfil all our patients' needs,' she said briskly, taking another sheet of paper out of her file. 'This is a list of our contacts at the local hospital. Obviously, you can request an appointment for a patient through the usual channels, but we find it speeds things up if we approach the head of each department on a personal basis.' She shrugged. 'A phone call is all it usually takes so it doesn't require that much extra effort.'

'It must add up, though.' Harry frowned as he took the sheet from her. 'I know how difficult it is to get hold of people so I doubt one phone call would do it. You must have to phone back several times.'

'Miles and I tend to make any phone calls after morning surgery finishes. That way we can catch people during their lunch-break and keep to our timetable.'

'I see.' Harry didn't say anything else as he placed the list on top of the other one. He was there to help, not to question how the practice was run. Nevertheless, he couldn't help thinking that it was no wonder Miles was so stressed when he was cramming so much into his day. Morning surgeries, evening surgeries, clinics, phone calls—he wouldn't have time to draw breath.

'How long do you allow for each consultation?' he asked, opting for a less controversial topic.

'We allocate ten minutes per patient, more if it's someone we know we will have to spend extra time with.'

'That's quite generous,' he observed, recalling what other GPs had told him recently. 'Most practices allow six minutes per patient and try to get away with less than that if they can.'

'We find it's a false economy to cut corners. If you don't

spend time getting to the root of a problem, invariably the patient ends up having to come back to see you.'

'It's a valid point, although I suppose it depends on how many patients you book in for each surgery,' he conceded, making a note to add it to his report. If more time was spent at the initial assessment stage then a second appointment might be avoided, and that was bound to be of help to an overworked GP. 'What's your maximum number of appointments per session?'

'We don't have a set limit. Both morning and evening surgeries are run on an open-door basis—in other words, if someone needs to see us they just turn up on the day.'

'But that's crazy. You could have the whole village turning up and have to see them.'

'I doubt it. Most people around here are too busy to waste their time by making unnecessary trips to see the doctor.' She shrugged. 'We find it works so I see no reason to change the routine. But if you find the pace too much for you, you only have to say so. I can deal with any patients you aren't able to see.'

'I am more than happy to do my share of the work,' he said flatly. He knew that she was trying to goad him but he wasn't going to fall into that trap again. No matter what Grace said or did from now on, he wasn't going to rise to the bait.

'Then we won't have a problem, will we?' She stood up and came around the desk, pausing as she drew level with him. 'Is there anything else you need to know? I think I've covered more or less everything to do with the day-to-day routine, but if there's anything you're not clear about then say so.'

'No, it all seems fairly straightforward.'

He stood up as well, feeling a tremor pass through him when his arm accidentally brushed against hers as he pushed back his chair. It immediately reminded him of what had happened the night before, and he sighed.

He still couldn't understand why that kiss had made such an impression on him. He'd been so afraid that Grace would notice something was wrong that he'd been desperate to get away. When Penny had assumed that he was going to look for that nurse, he hadn't bothered correcting her because it had seemed the easiest way to resolve his dilemma. Now, however, he found himself wishing that he hadn't let Grace believe that he was interested in the young woman. Maybe it was silly to be so sensitive but he wouldn't want her to think that he was more concerned with his love life than doing a good job here.

'Look, Grace, about that nurse last night—'

'Please.' She held up her hand, her beautiful mouth curling in distaste. 'Too much information, Harry. What you do in your free time is your business. I really don't want to hear all the gory details.'

She swept past him, leaving him feeling completely dumbfounded. Did she honestly think that he was crass enough to discuss his sex life with her? His spirits sank as he realised what a low opinion she must have of him. That he was more than partly to blame for it made him feel even worse. He should have put an end to their squabbling years ago.

Grace hurried into her consulting room and closed the door. She'd been dreading seeing Harry that morning and it had turned out to be every bit as bad as she'd feared. It had been hard enough to maintain her composure when he'd seen fit to criticise the way she and Miles ran the practice, but when he'd started to tell her about his nightly exploits with that nurse… Well!

Heat swept through her and she clutched hold of the doorknob. She didn't want to think about Harry's sex life but she couldn't seem to control the images that were crowding into her head, pictures of him and that nurse curled up in bed together—only it wasn't the nurse. She'd had blonde hair and the woman in her mind's eye had brown hair, caramel brown, just like hers...

Grace leapt away from the door and hurried to her desk. She must be more tired than she'd realised if she was dreaming up rubbish like that. It would be a cold day in hell before Harry Shaw got her into his bed.

She'd just switched on her computer when Janet, their receptionist, popped her head round the door to ask if she wanted a cup of coffee. Grace smiled gratefully. 'Yes, please. I didn't have time to make myself a drink before I left home this morning.'

Janet shook her head. 'You should eat a proper break-fast before you come into work. You need to keep your strength up. Why did you have to be here so early, anyway? I saw you drive past my house when I was fetching in the milk and it wasn't even eight o'clock at the time.'

Grace sighed as she realised that Janet had no idea what had happened to Miles. She quickly explained the situation to her, stressing the fact that Miles should make a full recovery when she saw how upset the reception-ist was. Everyone in the village loved Miles and she knew that a lot of people would be upset when they heard the news.

'So what are you going to do?' Janet asked, wiping away a tear. 'I mean, you can't manage all on your own. There's far too much work for just one person.'

'Which is why we've enlisted one of our friends to help until Miles is feeling better.'

Grace drummed up a smile, knowing that she couldn't let anyone suspect that she had doubts about working with Harry. If the patients had any inkling of how uneasy she felt about this alliance, they would have no confidence in Harry. 'Dr Shaw has offered to cover until Miles is feeling better, and I have to say that I think we're very lucky to have him. He's a superb physician and I know that our patients are going to receive the best possible care.'

She glanced up when a movement outside the door caught her attention, and blushed when she saw Harry was standing there, listening to what she was saying. He grinned at her as he came into the room, his blue eyes full of laughter and something else, something that made her feel all hot and shivery, as though she was running a fever. Having Harry look at her as though he was genuinely delighted by her comments was the last thing she'd expected. She wanted to run over to him and tell him that every word had been true, but how could she when she knew what he was really like?

Harry Shaw was a womanising Lothario. He didn't do anything unless it furthered his own career and brought him personal glory.

Grace made herself recite all the reasons why she disliked Harry but they no longer seemed to have the impact they'd had in the past. It all sounded very airy-fairy now, as though they were excuses, not genuine reasons. Did she truly believe that was all there was to Harry, or was she desperately trying to hold onto her old prejudices because she was afraid to face the truth? That Harry was a damned fine doctor who had worked incredibly hard to reach his present exalted position.

She didn't want to admit that she might have been wrong about him, but nothing seemed certain any more. The boundaries that had been drawn when they'd been students seemed to be breaking down, and Harry was no longer on one side and she on the other. For the next few weeks they would be working together as a team and, quite frankly, Grace didn't know how she was going to cope. She had a feeling that once Harry crossed that final boundary, her life would be changed for ever.

CHAPTER FOUR

'IF YOU would pop Bethany on the couch and take off her top and pants, I can examine her. I see from her notes that she was complaining of pains in her legs when you brought her in to see Dr Farrington at the beginning of December. How is she now?'

Harry pulled back the screen and waited while Mrs Clarke settled her daughter on the examination couch. Five-year-old Bethany looked very pale and listless as her mother undressed her.

'Much the same. She still keeps saying that her legs are sore. Dr Farrington said it was probably a virus because there were a lot of kiddies ill at the time with some bug or other. But it should have cleared up by now, I would have thought.'

'These things can take time to work themselves out of the system,' Harry explained, although it was unusual for a child to be ill for this length of time if it was only a viral infection. 'Can you just explain how it all started? I've read Bethany's notes but it's better to have a first-hand account, I find.'

'Well, it's like I said, Beth kept telling me her legs were hurting. I just assumed she'd hurt them when she'd been climbing the trees in our back garden so I didn't take that much notice at first.' Mrs Clarke sighed. 'She has three older brothers, you see, and she's always trying to copy them and getting into mischief.'

'A real little tomboy, are you, young lady?' Harry smiled at the little girl, although he had to admit that there didn't seem much sign of any mischief that day. Bethany appeared far too listless to cause any trouble. Bending down, he examined her legs, frowning when he saw that they were covered in bruises.

'How did she get all these bruises?' he asked, glancing at the mother.

'I've no idea. I only spotted them at the weekend. If she'd been playing outside, I would have assumed she'd fallen over and hurt herself, but she's not wanted to leave the house since Christmas.' Mrs Clarke stroked her daughter's hair. 'She keeps saying that she's too tired to play and it's just not like her. That's why I decided to bring her to the surgery again today. It's not natural for a child this age to be complaining that she's tired all the time, is it, Doctor?'

'Not if she's getting the right amount of sleep at night,' Harry agreed, moving to the top of the couch. He gently felt around Bethany's neck and under her arms, hiding his dismay when he discovered how enlarged the lymph nodes were in those areas. Although he would have expected to find some sign of enlargement if Bethany's body was fighting off an infection, this degree of swelling was unusual. It could be a sign that there was something seriously wrong with the child, although he didn't intend to rush to any conclusions. He would spend an extra few minutes checking the facts, as Grace had advised him to do.

The thought of Grace sent a rush of heat along his veins. He had to make a determined effort to ignore it as he carried on with his examination. 'Has Bethany complained of pain anywhere else, or have you noticed anything unusual happening recently?' he asked, trying not to dwell on how good it had felt to hear Grace praise him like that. He knew that in all likelihood it had been necessity that had prompted those comments: she'd wanted the receptionist to think that she was happy to work with him so it wouldn't cause any unrest within the practice. However, he couldn't deny that it had been a boost to his ego to hear her say something good about him for a change.

'Not really. It's been her legs mainly that she's been complaining about.'

'And there's been nothing else bothering her?' he insisted gently, sensing that the mother was holding something back.

'Well, it's probably nothing. I told her dad about it but he just said I was fussing so I wasn't going to mention it, but her gums have been bleeding. It's not just when she cleans her teeth either, which is why I thought it was a bit odd.'

Harry bit back a sigh. If he had a pound for every time a patient had thought it not worth mentioning a problem, he could have retired. 'I'm glad you told me, Mrs Clarke. It's important to have all the facts to hand when you're trying to diagnose what's wrong with a patient. Even something apparently trivial can help enormously.'

'I shall tell Brian that when I get home.'

Mrs Clarke looked pleased at having her concerns vindicated. She smiled at Harry, obviously expecting him to tell her what was wrong with her daughter and how he intended to put it right. Harry wished with all his heart it was that simple but, from what he had seen and heard so far, this problem wasn't going be resolved by writing out a prescription.

'I'd like to take a blood sample from Bethany, if you

wouldn't mind, Mrs Clarke. I'll send it off to the lab this morning and with a bit of luck we should have the results back before the end of the week.'

'A blood sample. Why ever do you need to do that? Dr Farrington never suggested it.'

'Dr Farrington didn't suggest it because at the time he didn't think it was necessary,' Harry said patiently. 'He assumed that Bethany's illness would clear up of its own accord, as most virus-related illnesses usually do. However, the fact that she is still complaining of feeling tired and that her legs hurt, and that there are other symptoms now, like the bruises and the bleeding from her gums, means that we need to investigate further. A blood test will help to point us in the right direction.'

'Well, I suppose it's all right if you think it's really necessary,' Mrs Clarke conceded, albeit reluctantly.

'I do.' He smiled encouragingly at her, hoping that his fears would prove to be groundless when the test results came back, although he doubted it. From what he had seen, this was one very sick little girl.

He quickly took the blood sample, praising the child when she didn't make a fuss about having the needle poked into her arm. He labelled the vial with her details then showed Mrs Clarke to the door.

'I'll get Janet to phone you when the results come back so we can arrange for you to call in and see me.'

'Right. Thank you, Doctor.'

The woman looked extremely troubled as she led her daughter down the corridor and Harry sighed. He hated to think that she was going to spend the next few days worrying herself to death, but it would have been remiss of him to voice his fears before he'd received confirmation that he was on the right track. Breaking bad news to a patient or a relative was never easy, and he realised all of sudden that he would welcome Grace's advice. After all, she knew the family and would have a better idea of how they would cope if his diagnosis proved to be correct.

He waited until surgery ended before he tapped on her consulting-room door. She looked up with a smile that faded when she saw him. Her voice was decidedly cool as she invited him in and, despite himself, Harry couldn't deny that it stung to have her treat him that way. She had the gift of making him feel like a pariah and it wasn't a pleasant experience.

'I just wanted a word with you about one of the patients,' he explained, opting for his most urbane tone, the one that made people think that nothing ever bothered him. It was a trick he'd learned early on in his life, and it had stood him in good stead over the years. With a bit of luck it would work like a charm now, too.

'My, my, I'm flattered, Harry. You're actually asking for my advice. Wow, that must be a first.'

She sat back in her seat, smiling up at him with eyes that were as warm as Arctic ice. Harry knew that he was more than partly to blame. He was the first to admit that he'd never done anything to improve the image she had of him. However, he couldn't help comparing her present response to what he'd overheard her saying earlier. If only Grace had meant all those lovely comments.

'They say there's a first time for everything,' he replied, chasing away that ridiculous idea. Hell would freeze over before Grace thought kindly of him.

'Indeed they do. So what can I do for you?' She glanced at her watch then arched a brow. 'I don't want to rush you, Harry, but I have a list of house calls to get through this afternoon.'

'Ah, the busy life you GPs lead,' he observed flippantly, knowing the remark was guaranteed to annoy her. He bit back a sigh when he saw her expression darken. It was stupid of him to behave this way when he needed her help.

'Sorry. That was uncalled for. I know how busy you are, Grace, so I won't waste your time. I wanted to ask you about the Clarke family. I assume you know them?'

'Yes, I do, although they're Miles's patients really.' She shrugged when he looked at her in surprise. 'Although we operate an open-door policy, we divide up the list so that people can see one or the other of us on a regular basis. They seem to prefer the idea of continuity of care.'

'I see. So Miles didn't mention anything about Bethany Clarke when her mother brought her in at the beginning of December?'

'Not that I can recall. Why? Is there a problem?'

'Everything is pointing that way, I'm afraid. Bethany has been complaining that her legs hurt. Miles assumed it was some sort of minor viral infection when he saw her. Apparently, a lot of the children had gone down with some sort of a bug at the time.'

'That's right. It did the rounds of the infants and the junior school.' Grace frowned. 'You're not saying that Miles misdiagnosed her, are you?'

'Of course not. We both know that Miles is a damned fine doctor and I certainly wasn't implying that he'd made a mistake.'

'I'm sorry.' Grace coloured as he glared at her across the desk.

'Me, too. I shouldn't have jumped down your throat like that.' Harry sighed roughly because he knew that he had overreacted. He had to stop looking for insults at every turn and just get on with the job.

'Anyway, I examined Bethany again today and I wasn't happy with what I found. Her legs are covered in bruises and the lymph nodes in her neck, groin and under her arms are massively enlarged. Her mother also told me that her gums have been bleeding and that she's been too tired to play outside.'

'You're thinking it could be leukaemia,' Grace said quietly.

'Yes. I'm afraid it could be.'

'I take it that you've ordered a blood test?'

'Yes. I'll get it sent off today. Hopefully we'll have the results back before the end of the week.'

'Mark it urgent,' she advised him. 'It costs more but it's worth it if you're right. We don't want there to be any delay in Bethany getting the treatment she needs.'

'I'll do that. What I need to know now is the best way to tell the parents. Are they the sort of people who can handle the facts, or would it be better if I tried a more roundabout approach?' He shrugged. 'Breaking bad news to people is never easy, and I don't want to make a mess of things.'

'I think they would appreciate it if you explained the situation to them in simple, straightforward terms. They're very down-to-earth people and not the kind who make a fuss. Obviously, if Bethany does have leukaemia, it will hit them hard, but they will cope with support from us and their families.'

'That's what I'll do, then.' He let out a huge sigh, unable to hide his relief. 'I feel better now that I have an idea how they will react. Normally, I've had time to get to know people before we reach this stage. It makes it easier to decide how to proceed.'

'It's never really easy, though. Telling someone that they have an illness that is going to affect their whole life is one of the most difficult things about our job.'

She smiled up at him, and Harry felt his heart race when he saw the sympathy in her eyes. In a blinding flash, he realised that she understood how he was feeling because she'd felt this way, too. To suddenly discover that Grace—prickly, feisty, oh-so-independent Grace—could empathise with him almost blew him away.

He had never experienced this kind of closeness with anyone before. Oh, he had friends by the dozen, colleagues by the score, but nobody had ever connected with him like Grace had done just now. It made him see that there was a bond between them that he had never even suspected.

'If there's anything else you need, just ask. I'm happy to help any way I can.'

Grace dredged up a smile but she could feel the back of her neck prickling with tension. She had never imagined that Harry would care so much about a patient. She had always assumed that he would be completely detached. However, there was no denying that he appeared genuinely concerned about Bethany and the effect her illness could have on her family.

'Thanks, Grace. I appreciate that.'

Harry returned her smile and she shivered when she felt goose-bumps break out all over her body. There seemed to be a new softness about his manner that she'd never seen before and, quite frankly, it scared her. She much preferred it when Harry behaved in the usual prescribed fashion because then she knew how to behave, too.

'Don't mention it,' she said briskly, standing up. 'It can't be easy, filling in for Miles. He's a hard act to follow, so if you have any more problems, let me know. I don't want you to feel that you're out of your depth while you're working here.'

'Thanks, but I think I can just about handle the job at a push.'

Grace hid her relief when she heard the edge that had

crept back into his voice. It was good to be back on familiar territory once more. 'Well, the offer's there if you need it,' she said sweetly.

After he'd left she collected up the notes she'd used during surgery and took them to the office, thinking about what had happened. It had been unsettling to see this new side to Harry but she mustn't let it upset her. So long as she maintained the status quo in the coming weeks, there shouldn't be a problem, although a lot would depend on Harry, of course. If he continued to throw surprises at her, it would make it that much more difficult. Perhaps that was what he was aiming for.

She frowned as she opened the office door. She had accepted his concern about Bethany at face value but had it been as genuine as she'd assumed it to be? Did she honestly believe that a self-serving, ambitious man like Harry cared two hoots about the little girl and her family?

Grace's mouth thinned as she realised how gullible she'd been. Leopards didn't change their spots. That little scene had been nothing more than a cunning ploy to knock her off balance. Harry had deliberately tried to gain her sympathy so that he would have the upper hand in the future. She would be less likely to go for the jugular if she thought he was a caring, sharing human being, but she wasn't going to fall for his tricks. Harry was Harry, and she wasn't about to make the mistake of thinking that he had suddenly turned into a saint.

She dumped her notes into the tray, scarcely able to believe that she'd allowed herself to be conned like that. Janet glanced up from her computer and grinned at her.

'Oh, dear, something seems to have upset you. What's happened?'

'Nothing. I'm fine,' Grace replied stiffly. Although she liked Janet, she didn't intend to discuss Harry with her.

Apart from the fact that it would be highly unprofessional, she couldn't trust herself not to say something she would regret.

'Well, it certainly doesn't look like it to me,' Janet replied cheerfully. 'What do you think, Harry? Wouldn't you say that Grace is looking rather stressed?'

'Hmm, I'm not sure if I'm the best person to ask.'

Grace swung round when she realised that Harry was standing behind her. He grinned at her as he deposited a pile of notes into the tray.

'I have a knack of rubbing Grace up the wrong way, so I'm not really in a position to judge. She usually looks stressed when I'm around, I'm afraid.'

'Really?' Janet was obviously intrigued by the remark. 'But I thought you two were old friends?'

'I'd like to think so but I'm not sure if Grace would agree with me.' He turned to her and Grace could see the challenge in his eyes. 'What do you think, Grace? Are you and I friends, or what?'

CHAPTER FIVE

HARRY knew it was probably a stupid thing to do. Asking a question like that was simply courting trouble, yet he desperately wanted to hear how she would describe their relationship. How could he and Grace have communicated as they had when discussing Bethany if they didn't even like each other? It didn't make sense.

'You'll be asking me next if I want to come over to your house for tea.' She smiled sardonically. 'Sorry, Harry, but I haven't felt the need for a best friend since I left junior school.'

'Really?' He folded his arms and regarded her thoughtfully, knowing that he should let the subject drop. He'd sworn that he wouldn't cause another argument so why was he pushing her? However, for some inexplicable reason, he knew that he needed to get to the bottom of what had gone on. 'So there isn't anyone you share your deepest, darkest secrets with?'

'I don't have any deep, dark secrets,' she enunciated very clearly. 'My life is very boring, and that's the way I like it.'

'I don't believe that.' Harry could tell that he was really pushing his luck. Grace was glaring at him now but he refused to give up. There had to be a logical explanation for the way they had connected before, and he wanted to know what it was.

'Everyone has secrets, Grace—even you. Things they share with the people they trust most of all, their closest friends.'

'And you're hoping that I'll share my secrets with you, are you, Harry?'

He shrugged nonchalantly, hoping she couldn't tell how much the thought appealed to him. 'If you want to.'

'I don't. Even if I had any secrets, you would be the last person I would share them with.'

She spun round on her heel and marched out of the room. There was a small pause before Janet said weakly, 'Oh, dear. That didn't go down too well. It's not like Grace to be so short with people.'

'It's my fault for winding her up. I knew it was the wrong thing to do,' Harry confessed. He sighed when Janet looked expectantly at him. 'Grace and I have a bit of a history, you see, and we usually end up sparring with each other.'

'Oh, I see.' Janet smiled. 'I thought it was odd for Grace to be so prickly. But if you two were an item at some point, then, that explains it. Still, I expect you'll work things out while you're here. And who knows what could happen?' she added archly, whisking the files out of the tray. 'You could discover that you still have feelings for one another.'

She disappeared into the back office before Harry could respond. He groaned as he sank down onto the chair she'd vacated. Janet obviously believed that he and Grace had been romantically involved at one time—an 'item', she'd called it—and nothing could be further from the truth.

He knew that he should go after her and explain, but he was afraid that he might cause more harm than good. Janet might think that he was trying to cover up his and Grace's supposed affair and that was the last thing he wanted. It might be better if he left well enough alone and simply hoped that Janet wouldn't say anything to Grace.

He groaned again because he could just imagine how Grace would react if she found out.

'I'd like you to come into the surgery for a proper check-up, Mr Bibby. These angina attacks are getting worse and I think we need to send you back to the hospital to see the consultant.' Grace rolled up her stethoscope and smiled at the elderly man. 'There's no point putting up with this level of discomfort if something can be done to help you, is there?'

'The pain has been getting worse,' Fred Bibby admitted. 'My Jeannie wanted me to pop in and see you before Christmas but I don't like to make a fuss. I know how busy you and Dr Farrington are. How is he, by the way? Mrs Roberts told me that he was taken poorly last night. Nothing too serious, I hope.'

'Angina, would you believe?' Grace explained, marvelling at how quickly the news about Miles had spread. Several of the people she'd been to visit that afternoon had asked after him so no doubt the whole village would know by teatime.

'Really? Why, he's just a young man. I must be double his age. I thought it was only old fellows like me as suffered with a dicky heart.'

'Unfortunately, a lot more younger men and women are experiencing heart problems,' Grace told him, trying not to think about the discussion she'd had with Harry the previous night on this very subject. She didn't want to think about Harry at all after what had happened in the office. She was still smarting from their last conversation. If Harry Shaw was the last man on earth, she wouldn't share any secrets with him.

'It's all this running around the young ones do. They seem to think they can work all the hours the good Lord sends then party all night.' Fred shook his head. 'I've heard what my Jeannie's lad gets up to and he runs himself ragged, I can tell you.'

'Is David still working in London?' Grace asked, relieved to direct her thoughts towards something other than Harry.

She closed her case and sat down on the settee. Fred had been on his own since his wife had died the previous year. Although his daughter, Jeannie, visited him every day, Grace knew that he was lonely. She made a point of spending an extra few minutes with him whenever she visited him, although undoubtedly Harry wouldn't approve. His interest in a patient probably only extended to their physical health, she thought scornfully.

'Aye. He's just bought himself this fancy apartment. Jeannie brought some photos round to show me. I suppose it's all right if you like that kind of thing but I'm too fond of my comforts. I don't much care for bare floors and all that white paint on the walls.'

Grace hid her smile. One glance around the cluttered farmhouse was enough to tell her that Fred's taste was vastly different to his grandson's. 'It sounds as though he's doing well, though. You must be very proud of him.'

'Oh, I am that. He's a good lad, never forgets to send me a card for my birthday and Christmas, and he phones me, too.' Fred sighed. 'I just wish he was interested in the farm. Once I go there'll be nobody to carry on running the place.'

'Maybe he'll change his mind,' Grace suggested, not wanting him to start feeling depressed.

'I can only hope. Anyway, enough of my problems. What about you, Dr Kennedy? How are you going to manage while Dr Farrington is poorly? Have you got another of them there locums to help you?'

'Actually, we've been extremely lucky. A friend of ours has offered to fill in while Miles is recuperating. Dr Shaw works in one of the big London hospitals. He's head of clinical care there, so we're very fortunate to have him on board,' she explained, doing her best to paint an attractive picture of her new partner.

The word 'partner' sent a jolt of alarm scudding through her and she frowned. She had never thought of Harry like that before, although that was what he was. He would act as her partner until Miles was well enough to return to work and the thought made her feel very on edge. There was something rather too personal, too intimate about the idea of having Harry as her partner.

She stood up, deciding it was time to bring her visit to an end before she got sidetracked. 'Ask Jeannie to bring you to the surgery, will you, Mr Bibby? I'll do an ECG and arrange for you to see a consultant.'

'Right, I'll do that. Thanks for coming, Dr Kennedy. It's much appreciated.'

'You're welcome.'

Grace saw herself out and hurried to her car. The weather had been bad when she'd set out at lunchtime and it had got steadily worse as the afternoon had progressed. Snow had been forecast for this part of Cumbria so she was glad that Fred Bibby was the last patient she had to see. Once the weather started to close in, the roads around the village became very treacherous, so it was a relief to be heading back to the surgery. She started the engine then groaned when her mobile phone rang. She could tell from the number on its display that the call was from the surgery, and that could only mean that Janet had another call for her to make.

'Hello, Janet, what's happened?' she asked briskly.

'It's not Janet, it's Harry,' a male voice announced.

Grace felt her heart bounce painfully against her ribs

before she managed to bring it under control. She wasn't going to get all steamed up because Harry had phoned her, she told herself sternly.

'Is there a problem?' she asked, pleased to hear that her voice sounded completely normal.

'Could be. We've had a call from Hilltop Farm. Apparently there's been an accident there. Janet has phoned for an ambulance but it will take almost an hour for it to get there.'

'I's not easy to get to the farm,' she agreed. 'And in weather like this, it could take even longer.'

'Which is why I've decided to go over there myself. We can't afford to wait for the ambulance if there's going to be a long delay. You know as well as I do that the first sixty minutes following an accident are crucial. Janet is worried that I might not be able to find the place, though. She suggested that I phone you so you could point me in the right direction.'

'Of course.' Grace was all business as she checked the clock on the dashboard. 'It's 3.15 now. I was just about to leave my last call and head back so I'll meet you on the bypass. There's a lay-by near the turn-off to the village. It should take me roughly ten minutes to get there. It's probably best if I go with you because I doubt you'll find the farm on your own.'

'Fine. I'll see you there.'

Grace put the phone back in its cradle. She had to admit that she was concerned about what Harry had told her. Hilltop Farm was a difficult place to get to even on a good day and if the ambulance didn't arrive, they could have a real problem on their hands.

A shiver ran through her and she quickly turned the car's heater to its highest setting before she set off. It was the chill that was getting to her, that was all. It had nothing to do with the thought of working with Harry. They might be partners but it was purely a temporary arrangement. In a couple of weeks' time he would return to London and she would carry on doing the job she loved here. Their lives would be restored to order and she, for one, would be glad to get back to normal.

The truth was that she much preferred it when Harry was at one end of the country and she was at the other. It was when he got too close that the problems started. What had he said to Janet earlier, that he rubbed her up the wrong way. Well, it was true. After a few minutes of Harry's company she was ready to do battle, and it wasn't like her to behave that way. She'd met other people she'd had little in common with but she'd never reacted to them the way she did to Harry. Was it just the fact that he reminded her of her errant father, or was there perhaps another reason why she behaved so completely out of character when he was around?

Grace tried to work it out but, as usually happened whenever she thought about Harry, her mind seized up. Perhaps she should accept that there was nothing rational about her feelings where Harry was concerned and leave it at that.

'How much further is it?'

Harry leant forward and peered through the windscreen. The weather had been getting steadily worse since Grace had met him on the bypass. The promised snowstorm had now arrived and the countryside was fast turning white. They had decided to travel to Hilltop Farm in Grace's car because it had four-wheel-drive and would be safer on the steep, winding roads than his own vehicle. However, he had to admit that he didn't enjoy being in the passenger seat when he was more used to taking charge.

'Just a couple more miles now. The farm's just over the next hill. You should be able to see it once we reach the top.'

She changed gear, easing the vehicle along the treacherous road surface. Harry shook his head in dismay. 'It's a hell of a place to get to.'

'It is. I only hope the ambulance makes it,' she said worriedly, glancing out of the window.

'Me, too,' he agreed, trying not to think about the problems it would cause if the ambulance didn't show up.

'Did you get any details at all about what had happened?'

'No. It was a child who phoned. He just said that there'd been an accident and they needed a doctor. He hung up before we could ask him any questions. Janet thought it was probably one of the farmer's grandsons.'

Grace nodded. 'Ben Arnold's son and his wife live on the farm as well. Ian and Jill have two boys so Janet was probably right. I wonder why one of the adults didn't phone the surgery, though.'

'I've no idea. Janet tried to phone him back but there was no reply.'

'I don't like the sound of this,' Grace said anxiously. 'Someone should have been there to answer the phone.'

They reached the top of the hill at last and she stopped the car and pointed through the side window. 'That's the farm over there. You can just make it out.'

Harry leant over so he could see out of the window. He felt a little flurry ripple along his veins when he suddenly inhaled the scent of her shampoo, something clean and fruity like the smell of crisp, green apples.

'There don't appear to be any lights on,' he said gruffly, because he didn't appreciate having something like that happen to him, right out of the blue. He'd already established that he wasn't attracted to Grace, so why did he feel so aroused whenever he was near her? It didn't make sense.

'No, there aren't. The whole place is in darkness. I don't like the look of this at all.'

Grace gunned the engine and set off down the other side of the hill. She seemed oblivious to his predicament, much to Harry's relief. It was bad enough to know that he was acting like a complete idiot but it would be ten times worse if Grace ever found out. He could just imagine what she would say if she discovered he was having all these lustful thoughts about her.

Grace turned the car onto a narrow track that led to the farm. She switched the headlights to main beam as she drew up in front of the farmhouse. 'Everywhere looks deserted. There's no sign of any lights in the house or in the yard.'

'No, there isn't,' Harry agreed grimly, pushing open the car door. He turned as Grace came to join him. 'I'm going to check out the barn. Can you have a look in the house and see if you can find anyone? There must be somebody around the place.'

'Will do. Here. You'd better take this.' She thrust a powerful torch into his hand then hurried towards the farmhouse, her feet slipping and sliding in the snow.

Harry waited until she was safely inside then made his way to the barn. He could hear cattle lowing but there was no other sound apart from the wind roaring down from the hills. Pushing open the door, he panned the beam of the torch around and jumped when several dozen pairs of eyes suddenly turned towards him. Obviously the cattle were expecting to be fed—they started kicking and stamping their feet, setting up a tremendous racket when they saw him. He hurriedly shut the door as Grace reappeared.

'Any sign of life in the house?'

'No. There's no one there and the electricity isn't working either. Do you think they've had a power cut?'

'It could explain the lack of lights.' He frowned. 'Maybe they're round the back of the barn, trying to rig up some sort of emergency lighting system. A lot of farmers have their own generators, don't they?'

'Yes, they do. But surely they would have heard us driving up the lane and come to investigate. And it still doesn't explain that phone call, does it?'

'No, although it could have been a hoax call. We haven't considered that possibility yet.' He shrugged when she looked at him in dismay. 'You know what kids are like, Grace. They think it's fun to have everyone racing around.'

'It would explain why there was no answer when Janet tried to phone back.' Grace sighed. 'Now I'm in a real dilemma. I don't know whether I'm annoyed at the thought or actually hoping it was just a stupid prank because it means that nothing awful has happened.'

Harry chuckled. 'The lesser of two evils, eh?'

'Something like that.'

She grinned up at him and once again he found himself reacting in a way he had never expected to do. This was Grace, he reminded himself as they set off round the barn. Grace whose sole aim in life since they'd been students together had been to prick and prod at him at every opportunity, to point out his flaws and poke holes in his achievements. She had been the bane of his life for more years than he could count, but for some reason that no longer seemed to matter. When he was with Grace now it was hard to think of her as anything other than a beautiful and very desirable woman.

CHAPTER SIX

GRACE could feel her anxiety mounting as she followed Harry along the rutted path past the barn. Maybe it had been a hoax call but she would feel happier once she knew what had happened to Ben Arnold and his family. They turned the corner and she gasped when a gust of wind almost blew her off her feet.

'Steady.'

Harry took a firm hold of her arm and held onto it as they made their way to the first of the outbuildings. Grace could feel the steady pressure of his fingers on her forearm and had to make a conscious effort not to pull away. He was just being polite, she told herself firmly, doing the gentlemanly thing by saving her from getting blown over. However, she was incredibly conscious of the solid bulk of his body as they made their way to the sheds.

'Nobody in here.' Harry shone the torch around the inside of the first shed. Grace frowned as she studied the rows of farming implements lined up around the walls.

'Ben would never go out and leave the place unlocked. Those tools cost a lot of money and he would make sure they were safely locked away.'

'It does seem odd,' Harry agreed. He moved away from

the shed and headed towards the next one then paused. 'Did you hear something?'

'Like what?' Grace demanded, stopping as well.

'I'm not sure. I thought I heard someone shouting… Yes, there it is again.'

He turned and ran towards the end of the path. Grace raced after him, her feet sliding on the slippery surface. They rounded the end of the row of outbuildings and she gasped at the sight that met them. There was a tractor lying on its side. When Harry shone the torch towards it she could see three bodies lying on the ground nearby. One of them was Ben Arnold and another was his son, Ian. The third person was a woman, although she couldn't tell if it was Sally Arnold, Ben's wife, or Jill, his daughter-in-law. There was also a young boy huddled against the back of the sheds; he looked up with tears streaming down his face.

'I can't wake them up. I've tried and tried but they won't talk to me.'

Grace ran forward and put her arms around him. 'It's all right now, darling, we'll look after them. Can you tell us what happened?'

'Dad and Granddad were outside, fixing the tractor, when there was this big bang and all the lights went out. Mum went out to see what had happened but she got hurt, too.' The child scrubbed his hands across his face. 'I tried to wake them up but they couldn't hear me. Gran took my brother Simon into town this afternoon so i was on my own. I didn't know what to do so I phoned the doctor.'

'You did exactly the right thing,' Grace assured him, as she gave him a hug. She glanced at Harry. 'What do you think has happened?'

'Possible electric shock, from the sound of it. It would certainly explain why the lights are out.' He studied the area around the tractor. 'Can you see a power cable anywhere about?'

'No, I can't,' Grace replied, although it was difficult to see anything with only the light from the torch to go by.

The boy stood up and pointed to a building close to the tractor. 'There should be an electricity cable attached to the top of the garage but I can't see it now. Maybe it's come loose.'

'I'm sure you're right,' Harry replied evenly although his expression was grim when he turned to Grace. 'We're going to have to be very careful in case the power is still switched on. The metal bodywork of that tractor will act as a conductor for the electricity so we can't afford to get too close in case the current arcs.'

'But we need to get those people away from there as quickly as possible,' she protested.

'I know that, but it doesn't mean we should go rushing in, unprepared.' He turned to the boy. 'What's your name, son?'

'Steven,' the boy told him, shivering from a combination of cold and shock.

'Right, Steven, my name is Harry and I'm a doctor just like Dr Kennedy. We want to help your mum and dad, and your granddad, too, but to do that we're going to have to move them to somewhere safe. What we really need is something we can use to drag them away from that tractor, but it mustn't be anything that's made of metal. Do you know if there's any long pieces of wood around here we could use?'

Steven nodded eagerly. 'There's some old fence posts in one of the sheds.'

'Great, that's just what we need. Can you show me where they are?' He turned to Grace. 'Don't go any closer. Just stay here until I get back with that wood.'

'Be as quick as you can,' she said, glancing worriedly at the people lying on the ground.

'I will.'

Harry squeezed her shoulder then hurried after the child. Grace huddled into the shelter of the outbuildings as they disappeared. The wind was bitterly cold as it blew along the gap between the buildings; she could feel her hands and feet going numb. She couldn't bear to imagine how Ben and his family must be suffering, lying on the snow-covered ground, so it was a relief when Harry returned a few minutes later, carrying several sturdy lengths of wood.

'I'm going to try to drag then away from that tractor. I can't see any sparks coming from where that power cable must have fallen so the electricity might have been switched off, but there's no point taking any chances.'

He started towards the tractor but Grace grabbed hold of his arm. 'Wait—aren't you supposed to insulate yourself so you don't come into contact with the ground?'

'Yes. Fortunately, I'm wearing rubber-soled shoes so they should minimise the risk.'

'Oh, right. I see.' Grace bit her lip. They had to move the family so they could help them but she couldn't pretend that she wasn't worried about Harry putting himself at risk this way.

'I'll be fine, Grace. Stop fussing.'

His tone was brisk and had the immediate effect of making her feel rather foolish. Harry was a grown man, for heaven's sake. He didn't need her mothering him.

She didn't say anything else as he carefully made his way across to where the first casualty, a woman, was lying. Using the piece of wood, he managed to drag her away from the tractor. Grace hurried forward as soon as he signalled it was safe to do so and knelt beside her. It was Jill Arnold, and she was unconscious but breathing and her pulse was strong. The only visible sign of injury was a lump on the back of her head. Grace took off her coat and covered her with it then turned to Steven who was standing nearby.

'Can you run back to the house and find some blankets? Your mum is very cold from lying on the ground and we need to warm her up.'

She got up as the child hurried away and turned to see what Harry was doing. He had succeeded in moving Ian away from the tractor but the young man was a lot heavier than his wife and Harry was having problems moving him a safe distance from the vehicle with only the aid of a piece of wood.

Grace picked up a second piece of wood and went to help, shaking her head when he looked as though he was going to protest. 'Before you say anything, I'm also wearing rubber-soled shoes so I'm as safe as you are.'

He didn't say anything to that. However, his expression was grim as she helped him manoeuvre the young man closer to the outbuildings. As soon as they were far enough away from the tractor, he dropped the wood and dragged Ian the rest of the way and laid him down beside his wife.

'You stay here and look after them while I fetch the other guy,' he instructed in a tone that brooked no argument.

'Just be careful.' Even though Grace had sworn she wouldn't make a fuss, she couldn't help worrying about him. 'You'll be closer to the power cable this time so mind what you're doing.'

Harry cocked a mocking brow. 'Carry on like that, Grace, and I'll start to think that you care about me.'

Grace flushed hotly. Nobody had ever managed to get under her skin the way Harry could. 'Dream on. If I appear concerned, it's because I don't want to have another casualty on my hands.'

'And here was I thinking that you cared.'

He treated her to one of his most infuriating smiles then made his way over to where Ben was lying. Grace turned away, busying herself with tending to Ian. The devil looked after his own, or so the saying went, and no doubt Harry would be perfectly safe.

She stole a glance over her shoulder and breathed a sigh of relief when she saw that he had managed to move the older man away from the source of danger without any mishap. She turned her attention back to the young farmer, checking his airway, breathing and circulation—the ABC of first aid. She would do the job she was trained to do and leave the heroics to Harry. No doubt he would enjoy the opportunity to cover himself in yet more glory.

CHAPTER SEVEN

'HERE'S the exit wound. The current must have entered his body through his right hand and exited via his left foot.'

Harry frowned as he examined Ben Arnold's foot. The flesh was charred and blackened, and it looked as though at least two of his toes had been damaged beyond repair. It was going to take some very skilled surgery to sort out the mess, although it was unlikely to be the only injury the farmer had suffered.

'It's the worst type of electrical injury. When the current travels diagonally through the torso, it can pass through the heart. I think that must have happened in this case because Ben's exhibiting definite signs of cardiac arrhythmia.' Grace looked equally concerned as she glanced up. 'The really worrying thing is that there's no way of assessing the full extent of any internal damage. There could be wide-spread destruction of tissues and major organs for all we know.'

'There could also be bone fractures.' Harry grimaced. 'Remember that case we saw when we were students—the fifteen-year-old who'd been messing about on the railway track and touched the live cable. I couldn't believe it when we were shown his X-rays. He'd broken so many bones it was like looking at a jigsaw puzzle.'

'The senior registrar told us it was because he couldn't let go of the cable. As the current passed through his body it caused spasmodic contractions of his muscles, making it impossible for him to release the cable. The severity of the shocks caused joint dislocations as well as fractures, and it didn't help that he'd been thrashing about on the ground as well.' She shuddered. 'It was a really horrible case. It's no wonder you remember it.'

'It's not something you could forget in a hurry,' Harry agreed. 'He also had a severe case of concussion, as I recall. The registrar reckoned the convulsions had been so strong that his brain had been rattling about inside his skull—like the damage you see in shaken-baby syndrome. It means we can't rule out a head injury in this instance either.'

'No, we can't.' Grace sat back on her heels. 'I don't think I've ever felt so helpless in my entire life. Ben could have suffered any number of injuries and it's hard to know where to start for the best.'

'Let's take it one step at a time and deal with the problems we know about,' he advised, trying to hide his surprise. It simply wasn't like Grace to admit to feeling unsure of herself when he was around. She always made a point of being very much in control of the situation—rather like he did, in fact.

Harry frowned. It was almost as big a surprise to realise that he, too, made a point of putting on a good show whenever they were together. He wasn't sure why he felt it necessary to prove himself when he was with her. It certainly wasn't something he did as a matter of course. Although he wasn't arrogant enough to think that he knew everything there was to know about medicine, he was confident of his own abilities and knew that the people he worked with had confidence in him, too. However, when Grace was around, he felt that he had to make a special effort to impress her. How strange.

It was all very puzzling and he was glad to put it out of his mind when Steven arrived with a pile of blankets. 'Well done—that's just what we need. Here, help me cover up your mum then you can sit with her while we look after your dad and your granddad.'

He removed Grace's coat from Jill Arnold and helped the boy spread a blanket over her then sat him down beside her. 'Now I want you to hold her hand so she knows you're here.'

'She's not going to die, is she?' Steven asked haltingly.

'No, she's not.' Harry crouched down beside him. 'Listen—can you hear her breathing?' He smiled when the boy nodded. 'Good. Now put your fingers on her wrist just here—that's it. Can you feel her pulse beating? Well, that means her heart is working as well and that she isn't in any immediate danger.'

'Why won't she wake up, then?' the boy asked, his fingers still firmly clamped around his mother's wrist.

'I don't know, Steven, because I don't really know what happened to her,' Harry admitted truthfully. 'We can't find any burn marks on her so it doesn't look as though she came into contact with the electric current, but we won't know for sure until we get her to hospital.' He ruffled the boy's hair. 'If you can sit there and make sure you can hear her breathing, though, it will be a big help.'

He left the child and went back to Grace. She was still kneeling beside Ben and he saw her shiver as a flurry of snow blew off the shed roof and landed on top of her.

'Here's your coat,' he said, quickly handing it to her.

'Thanks.' She stood up and shrugged it on then crouched down again.

'How's he doing?' Harry asked, kneeling beside her and trying not to think about what he had just seen. Getting hung up on the thought of Grace's delectable body was the last thing he needed. He had to keep a clear head so he could concentrate on what he was doing, yet it was hard to ignore the images that were flickering across his mind's eye: the lushness of her breasts; the narrowness of her waist; the enticing curve of her hips…

'Not too good. I don't like the sound of his breathing and his pulse is all over the place…' She broke off and pressed her fingers against Ben's neck. 'He's arrested.'

'Damn,' Harry rolled the man over onto his back. He glanced at Grace. 'Check again that there's no output, will you?'

Grace placed her fingers on the man's neck once more, positioning them in the hollow between his larynx and the adjoining muscle so she could check his carotid artery. She waited for a moment then shook her head. 'No. There's definitely no pulse.'

'Right. I'll do the compressions while you do the breathing.'

'Fine.'

She quickly positioned the man's head so that his airway was open, using her hand to support the back of his neck while she tilted his head back. Once he was positioned correctly, she gave four sharp inflations then checked to see if there was a pulse. 'Still nothing,' she told Harry tersely.

Harry placed his hands on the man's chest and pushed down five times, adjusting the rhythm to equal sixty compressions per minute. He paused after a minute while Grace checked again for any output then carried on when she shook her head. They must have completed several dozen cycles before she suddenly ordered him to stop.

Harry sank back onto his heels as she checked Ben's pulse once more. He could feel sweat trickling down his neck and running between his shoulder blades. It was hard work resuscitating a patient and despite the cold weather he'd built up a real sweat.

'Yes!' Grace looked up and grinned at him. 'We've got a pulse.'

'Hallelujah,' Harry muttered, almost too exhausted to speak.

She laughed. 'You must be going soft in your old age, Harry. A couple of years ago you'd have been able to keep going for a lot longer than that.'

'If you're trying to say that I'm getting old, I would have to agree with you.' He staggered to his feet, exaggerating his fatigue because it was just so good to know that she could share a joke with him. Normally, she laughed *at* him not *with* him, and he couldn't deny how wonderful it felt to have crossed the line and feel like a friend instead of an enemy.

'None of us is getting any younger,' he said, clutching his back and hamming it up for all he was worth. 'You might feel that you're on top of the game at the moment but you'll soon discover what it's like, young lady.'

'That might be true, but I'll always be younger than you, Harry,' she retorted sweetly.

Harry rolled his eyes. 'You call six months being younger? Oh, please!'

'Now, now, don't get snippy.' She picked up a blanket and tucked it around the farmer. 'Just because you'll be drawing your pension before me isn't an excuse to throw a tantrum.'

'I give up.' Harry shook his head in mock despair. 'Obviously, I'm not going to win this argument so I may as well save my breath.'

'It's always best to know when you're beaten, Harry.'

'Is that a fact?'

He grinned wolfishly back at her, scarcely able to believe that they were having this conversation. Why, if he didn't know better he'd think that Grace was actually flirting with him.

The thought sent a buzz of heat through his body. He was already hot from his recent exertions and maybe the extra surge of heat forced his brain into overload because he didn't even pause to consider the wisdom of what he was doing. If Grace was flirting with him then there was no way that he was going to let the occasion pass him by.

'The one thing I never do is accept that I'm beaten. You might have won this particular round, Dr Kennedy, but I'll get even at some point. You can be sure of that.'

Grace felt a little thrill of excitement course through her. There had been something in Harry's voice when he had issued that threat that made her feel all warm and tingly inside...

She turned away, realising how stupid it was to lower her guard like that. Opening her case, she took out a bag of saline, steadfastly ignoring Harry as she set up a drip. She needed to get herself back onto an even keel, although it wasn't going to be easy. She had never flirted with a man before today, and had never wanted to either. Although she still went out on the occasional date, she always made it clear that she wasn't interested in anything more than friendship. Few men asked her out a second time. Most were put off by her attitude, but it didn't worry her.

She had her career and her friends and they'd been more than enough to fill her life up till now, so why had she behaved that way with Harry, of all people? Harry was the master when it came to sexual shenanigans—what he didn't know about seducing a woman would fit on a postage stamp. And she had just declared herself fair game.

Grace forced down her groan of dismay. There was no way that she was going to let Harry know how much she regretted her actions. 'Ben's stable now so we'd better check on Ian.'

'We'd better check where that ambulance has got to as well.' Harry checked his watch. 'It should have been here by now.'

'I just hope it hasn't got stuck somewhere along the way,' Grace replied, relieved to hear him sounding so normal, although what had she expected? That he would try and hit on her right here in the middle of the farmyard? No, that wasn't Harry's style, he was far too skilled in the art of seduction to make such a basic error. He would wait for a more appropriate opportunity to present itself.

The thought wasn't exactly soothing but there was nothing she could do about it right then. She would just have to deal with the situation if and when it arose. 'Why don't you get onto Ambulance Control and ask them for an update?' she suggested, making her way across to Ian.

'That's what I was going to do.' Harry took his mobile phone out of his pocket then groaned. 'Damn, there's no signal here. I'll have to walk back up to the farmhouse and use the phone in there.'

'It's in the kitchen near the back door,' Grace told him.

'Thanks. I'll find it.'

She knelt down beside Ian as Harry hurried away, relieved to see that he had started to regain consciousness. 'Hi, Ian. How are you feeling?' she asked as she checked his pulse.

'I dunno... What's happened?' He lifted his head and gazed around in confusion. 'Why am I lying outside in the yard?'

'You've had an accident. We think you must have suffered an electric shock,' she explained, removing the dressing she had put on earlier so she could check his right thigh. From the burn marks, it appeared that the current had entered Ian's body through his thigh and passed out through his foot. Although he wasn't as badly burned as his father, she knew that he could have suffered quite substantial damage to the limb.

'An electric shock,' Ian repeated blankly.

'Hmm. Steven said there was a power cable attached to the top of the garage. We think that must have been the cause of the accident.'

Ian gasped. 'I remember now. Dad was working on the tractor—the engine kept cutting out—but he managed to fix it. I was just taking the tools he'd used back to the shed when I noticed the cable had come loose. I turned round to warn Dad to be careful when he put the tractor away and there was this massive bang and all the lights went out.'

'Ben must have hit the power cable somehow,' Grace said, trying to hide her dismay when she saw how swollen Ian's leg looked.

'He must have done, although I didn't think of that at the time. I just saw him lying on the ground and I suppose I panicked,' Ian admitted. 'I remember running towards him, then there was this blinding flash of light and I don't remember anything else after that.'

'The current must have arced and struck you as well,' she said, checking his ankle to see if she could detect a pulse.

'It must have done…' He broke off and groaned. 'My leg really hurts. It feels like it does when you get a cramp when you're swimming, only ten times worse.'

'I think you might be suffering from something called compartment syndrome,' Grace explained calmly, trying not to alarm him. There was no pulse in his ankle, which meant that his circulation had been severely compromised.

'What's that when it's at home?' Ian asked, grimacing.

'It means that the muscles in your leg have swollen so much that the arteries are being compressed and the blood can't pass through them.'

'Well, whatever's causing it, it bloody well hurts…'

'I know,' she soothed lightly. She stood up when Harry appeared and nodded towards the shed to indicate that she needed a word with him. He looked very grim after she finished telling him about her concerns.

'If it is compartment syndrome, we need to get him to hospital a.s.a.p. or he could lose the leg.'

'He could lose it anyway if there's been sufficient necrosis,' she pointed out. 'What's happening about that ambulance? Is it on its way?'

'Yes, but there's a problem, apparently. It can't get up the hill because of the snow so it's had to turn back. Ambulance Control wants us to ferry the injured down to the road and meet the paramedics there. They're going to despatch a second ambulance because of the number of casualties.'

'It's all very well for them to suggest that but we have no idea how severe their injuries are. We can't just stuff everyone into the car and hope for the best.'

'I understand what you're saying, Grace, but, realistically, what choice do we have? We can keep them here and hope the weather improves, which seems highly unlikely, or we can get them to the ambulances so they can be taken to hospital.'

'It's hardly ideal, though,' she muttered, although she knew he was right. The longer treatment was delayed, the more danger Ben and his family would be in.

'No, it isn't ideal. And if I had a magic wand, I would conjure up a whole fleet of ambulances with snow-ploughs attached to their fronts and chains on their tyres, but I'm not that talented.' He placed his hands on her shoulders and gave her a gentle shake. 'We can't perform magic, Grace, but we can do our level best to help these people. So are you willing to work with me and give it your very best shot?'

CHAPTER EIGHT

HARRY held his breath. It was vital that Grace saw the sense of what he was suggesting, although he knew it wasn't the only reason he wanted her to agree. If she accepted that he was right about this, it could mean that she was willing to trust him. And that would mark a turning point in their relationship.

'All right. As you say, I don't think we have much choice.'

It was hardly the most gracious capitulation but he was too buoyed up to argue about it. He smiled at her, unable to hide his delight. 'Great.'

He gave her shoulders a quick squeeze then stepped back before he got too carried away. She may have conceded that he was right to ferry the casualties to the ambulances, but it would be madness to make the mistake of thinking that she was ready to fall into his arms.

'Can you fetch your car round here?' he questioned, deeming it wiser to focus on the logistics of the exercise. 'It will be easier than trying to move everyone over to where it's parked.'

'Of course.' Grace turned away then paused. 'We won't be able to fit all three of them in at once so we need to decide who is the most seriously injured.'

'It's a tough call but I think Ian should be the first to

go.' Harry glanced at the young farmer. 'The sooner something is done about that leg of his, the better.'

'I agree. How about we take Ian and Jill, then? I doubt if we'll be able to fit both the men in—they're too big. We should be able to get Jill in as well as Ian, though.'

'Sounds fine to me.'

Harry didn't waste time debating the issue. Someone would have to be left behind for now and it looked as though it was going to have to be Ben. He went over to young Steven as Grace hurried away, and crouched down beside him.

'Dr Kennedy's going to drive your mum and dad down to the main road. The ambulance can't get up here because of the snow so we're going to take them down in her car to meet it. I'll stay here with your granddad and we'll move him later.'

'Can I go with them?' Steven asked anxiously.

'I can't see why not. We should be able to squeeze you in somehow or other.'

Harry stood up when Grace returned with the car. She parked beside them then jumped out and ran round to the back to open the tailgate.

'I'll drop the rear seats so we can lay Ian and Jill down flat in the back. They'll be more comfortable that way.'

'Good idea,' Harry agreed, going over to help her.

As soon as they had cleared enough space, they made their way to where Ian was lying. 'Ian, we're going to take you and Jill down to the main road,' he explained. 'The ambulance can't get up here because of the snow so it's the fastest way we can think of to get you both to hospital.'

'Take my dad first,' Ian protested, although it was obvious that he was in a great deal of pain.

'It's better if you go first,' Grace said gently. 'Your dad is quite badly injured, but he's stable at the moment. Harry and I both feel that you need to get that leg seen to as soon as possible or you could lose it.'

Ian blanched. 'I didn't realise it was that serious.'

'It is, which is why we need you to work with us,' Harry said firmly.

He stood up and helped the younger man upright. With Grace's help they managed to get Ian into the car. Harry sorted out some pain relief for him then they went to fetch Jill. She had recovered consciousness and looked very shaken when he explained what had happened.

'Did you get an electric shock?' he asked, once he was sure she understood what was going on.

'No. I realised what had happened as soon as the lights went out so I switched the power off at the mains.' She raised a tentative hand to her head. 'I slipped on the ice as I was running across the yard and must have knocked myself out.'

'Well, it must have been a hefty blow because you've been unconscious for a while. That means it's very important that we get you to hospital so the doctors can check you over.' He glanced at Steven and smiled. 'Your son's been a big help. He phoned the surgery and he's been keeping an eye on you while we've been looking after the others. You should be really proud of him.'

Jill's eyes filled with tears as she squeezed her son's hand. 'I am.'

'He's done wonders,' Grace concurred, taking a cervical collar out of her case and fitting it around Jill's neck. 'A lot of children would have panicked but Steven's been really brave. He's going to have a lot to tell his older brother.'

Jill gasped. 'Simon… I was supposed to pick him up from the swimming baths at four o'clock.'

Harry glanced at his watch. 'It's gone four already. Is there anyone else who could collect him?'

'My mother-in-law. She's gone into the village to have her hair done. Could you phone the hairdresser's and tell her what's happened? I can't remember the number but it should be in the phone book.'

'Don't worry. We'll sort it all out,' Grace assured her. She glanced at Harry. 'How do you want to do this?'

'I'd feel happier if Jill remained lying flat to minimise the risk in case there's any spinal damage. Unfortunately, it means we're going to have to carry her to the car.' He turned to Steven. 'What we need is some kind of a board to put under your mum. Is there anything in the sheds we could use?'

'Yes. Dad made me a toy garage for Christmas and there was a big piece of wood left over.' The boy jumped up. 'I'll show you where it is.'

The piece of fibreboard was ideal for their purposes. With Steven's help they managed to carry Jill to the car and place her alongside her husband. Harry helped the boy into the passenger seat then opened the driver's door so Grace could get in.

'Take your time going down that hill. It was bad enough when we drove up here, and it will be ten times worse now with all this snow.'

'I'll be fine,' she assured him, fastening her seat belt. 'I'll be back as soon as I can for you and Ben.'

'OK. But take care.'

Harry slammed the door because there wasn't time to linger over his goodbyes. The sooner Jill and Ian reached the ambulance, the sooner they would be on their way to hospital. However, as he watched the car's taillights disappear up the track, he couldn't help feeling anxious. He couldn't bear to think that Grace might be placing herself at risk when what he really wanted to do was to protect her.

* * *

'Thanks, Janet. If you can phone the baths and ask one of the staff to tell Simon his grandmother is on her way to collect him, that would be a big help. We've just about finished here so we should be back at the surgery very shortly.'

Grace switched off her phone and stowed it in her pocket. Harry was having a final word with the crew from the second ambulance. Jill and Ian were already on their way to hospital and Ben would soon be following them. All things considered, everything had worked out extremely well and it was mainly thanks to Harry. She wouldn't have managed half as well if he hadn't been there to help her.

She sighed as she made her way over to him. Twenty-four hours ago she would have laughed if anyone had suggested that she would be glad of his help, which just went to show how much truth there was to the old line, 'What a difference a day makes.' Harry wasn't just the self-serving glory-seeker she'd believed him to be but a damned fine doctor who responded well in a crisis. There was more to Harry than she'd given him credit for, and she wasn't sure if she was comfortable with the idea.

'That's it.' He turned and smiled at her as the ambulance drove away. 'I'd say it was a job well done, wouldn't you?'

'I suppose so.' She shrugged, not wanting him to guess how uneasy she felt about having to readjust her ideas. She'd learned through experience that the best way to deal with Harry was to keep him at arm's length, but it would be far more difficult to do that if she kept finding things to admire about him.

'You *suppose* so?' He glowered at her. 'We just helped to save three people's lives. Now, that might not be a big deal to you but it is to me.'

'Of course I'm pleased that Ben and his family are going to receive the treatment they need, but the day isn't over yet,' she retorted. 'We have a surgery full of patients waiting for us so I suggest we leave the back-slapping until later.'

'Don't you ever lighten up?'

'I've no idea what you mean,' she said crisply, walking towards her car. Harry had left his car in the lay-by and she would have to give him a lift back there, although she could have done without spending any more time with him. As she knew to her cost, a little of Harry went a very long way.

'Of course you know what I mean.' He slid into the seat beside her. 'You never relax, do you, Grace? You were the same at med school. When everyone else was out having fun, you were the one who stayed behind to study.'

'You did enough socialising for all of us,' she shot back, fastening her seat belt.

Harry laughed. 'I didn't go out more than anyone else in our year did. It was just some crazy misconception of yours that I spent all my time partying.'

'Really, and what about all those women you dated? Were they another of my misconceptions?'

'OK, so I had a lot of dates.' He held up his hands. 'But no more than any other guy in our year.'

'Oh, come on, the list of your conquests was the stuff of legend. Every single guy on campus envied you.'

'I don't know why. At least when most of them asked a girl for a date, they knew why she'd agreed to go out with them. It was never that simple for me.'

'What do you mean by that?' she asked in surprise.

'That a lot of the girls I went out with weren't particularly interested in me as a person. It was the package they fancied more.'

'The package?'

'Uh-huh.' He turned and looked at her. 'What was the first thing you thought when you met me, Grace?'

'What a stupid question. How on earth can I remember after all this time?' she protested, although it wasn't true. She remembered exactly what she'd thought when she'd met Harry because he had epitomised everything she disliked in a man—rich, handsome, sure of himself and the effect he had on a woman.

'OK, then I'll tell you what you thought. You thought I was a rich guy on the way up. I don't blame you because it's what most women think when they meet me. They don't look beyond the outward trappings because they're not interested in what I think or how I feel. They're only interested in what I can give them.'

'That's a horrible thing to say.'

'Yes. But it's true.' He sighed heavily. 'Take that nurse last night, for instance. She wasn't really interested in me. All she saw was a guy who wasn't too hideous-looking and who had enough money to show her a good time.'

'You didn't exactly fight her off, though,' she retorted, although the comment had surprised her. Did Harry really believe that the women he went out with were more interested in his financial status than him?

'I know you won't believe this, Grace, but I did *not* hit on her. Hell, I was too worried about Miles to think about anything else. She was the one who came onto me, not the other way round.'

'But you still made a date with her,' she pointed out, determined to restore some balance to the picture of innocence he was painting.

'No, I didn't.'

'But you told Penny and me that you were going to find her.'

'No. You both assumed that was what I was going to

do, and I didn't bother to correct you.' He shrugged. 'The truth is I'm tired of being seen as a commodity. If I go out with a woman from now on, I want to know that she's interested in me, not what I can give her. I've had my fill of meaningless affairs and now I want something more. I suppose what I'm really saying is that I'm happy to trade meaningless sex for the chance of a proper relationship.'

'Please, sit down.'

Harry waited while the woman took a seat. Elaine Ledbetter was his last patient of the day and he had to admit that he was glad to get to the end of the list. It had been an extremely busy day and he didn't seem to have had a minute to himself since he'd got up that morning. No wonder poor Miles had ended up in hospital if this was an example of the pressure he'd been under recently, he thought as he brought up Elaine Ledbetter's notes onto the computer screen. Although at least Miles didn't have to suffer Grace's constant nit-picking.

The thought of Grace was far too unsettling. Harry couldn't help wishing that he hadn't told her all that stuff earlier. He'd never meant to pour out his heart to her but that's what he'd done. What had made it worse was that she obviously hadn't believed him. Even though she hadn't said a word at the time, he'd been able to tell from her expression that she didn't think he was capable of having a proper relationship with a woman, and maybe she was right, too.

After all, what basis did he have for thinking that he had the staying power to commit to one woman for the rest of his life? He'd never been out with any woman more than half a dozen times. Usually, he was so bored by then that he couldn't wait to end it. His friends often accused him of having a cavalier attitude towards women, but it wasn't true. He always made sure that every woman he dated knew not to expect more from him than some excellent nights out—and in. His inability to commit had never been a problem in the past, but it would be different if he asked someone to share his life. He would have to give part of himself in a relationship like that and he wasn't sure if he was capable of doing that.

It wasn't often that Harry felt lacking in any respect and he didn't appreciate the feeling now. He pushed the thought to the darkest corner of his mind and smiled at his patient. 'I'm Harry Shaw. I'm standing in for Dr Farrington while he's off sick.'

'It's nice to meet you, Dr Shaw. I heard what had happened to poor Dr Farrington—not that I was surprised, mind you. Dr Farrington and Dr Kennedy both work far too hard.'

'It's a very busy practice,' Harry agreed, not wanting to think about Grace again. Maybe she didn't believe he was capable of making a commitment to just one woman, but it was his decision, not hers. 'So, Mrs Ledbetter, can you tell me what the problem is today?'

'It's my ears, Dr Shaw.' The attractive fifty-year-old sighed. 'I keep getting this horrible buzzing sound in my left ear. It feels as though there's pressure in it, too—like when you're on a plane and you're waiting for your ears to pop.'

'I see.' Harry took the otoscope off the desk and stood up. 'I'd like to examine both your ears. Have you noticed any discharge from either ear or pain that could indicate an infection?'

'There's been some discharge and pain in my left ear,' Elaine admitted, pushing back her hair.

'Right.' He examined her ear, using the magnifying lens of the otoscope to check the ear canal and the eardrum. Owing to the semi-transparent nature of the eardrum it was possible to see right into the middle ear, though there didn't appear to be any obvious sign of infection present.

'That looks clear enough,' he said, moving round so he could check her right ear next. There was no sign of infection in that ear either so he switched off the otoscope and sat down. 'Is your hearing impaired at all?'

'Yes. Everything sounds muzzy, especially in my left ear—it's as though I'm listening to everything underwater.' Mrs Ledbetter took a quick breath then rushed on. 'My mother had Ménière's disease and I'm terrified it might be that, Dr Shaw.'

'Ménière's disease can be extremely distressing,' Harry agreed sympathetically. 'As well as suffering from hearing loss and tinnitus—that's the name for all those noises people hear in the affected ear—there's the problem of vertigo. It can be very debilitating.'

'Mum was really bad with it,' Elaine explained sadly. 'Sometimes the dizzy spells lasted for almost a week, and there was nothing she could do except wait for them to pass.' She shuddered. 'I don't know if I'd be able to cope if I ended up like that.'

'But you haven't had an attack of vertigo, have you?'

'No, although I felt a bit giddy when I bent down to put on my shoes this afternoon. Does that mean it is Ménière's?'

'It's quite common to feel dizzy if there is something wrong with your ears. Even a fairly minor infection can disturb your balance so let's not jump to any conclusions.' Harry picked up a tuning fork and showed it to her. 'I'm going to test your hearing with this. I'll place it near the opening of your ear first of all, then do it again with the base of the fork against the mastoid bone, which is the bit just behind your ear. I want you to tell me where the sounds are loudest.'

He showed Elaine where he would place the tuning

fork so that she knew what to expect then rapped the instrument on the desk. It emitted a high-pitched hum as he held it beside her right ear.

'I can hear that,' she told him.

'How about behind the ear?' he asked, rapping the tuning fork again and placing the end on the mastoid bone. 'Is the sound louder or quieter?'

'Quieter.'

'Good. Now let's repeat the procedure with your left ear.'

This time Elaine didn't fare as well; she couldn't hear the sound when the tuning fork was held against her ear, although she could hear it when it was placed behind it.

'Why could I only hear the sound when the tuning fork was placed behind my ear?'

'Almost all sound is heard by a process called air conduction. Sound waves travel through the air and the pinna—that's the visible part of your ear—channels them along the auditory canal to the eardrum. Sound waves of different frequencies cause the eardrum to vibrate at different speeds and these vibrations are conveyed to the inner ear. They're then converted to nerve impulses, which are transmitted to the brain.'

'Good heavens!' Elaine exclaimed. 'I never realised how complicated your hearing is.'

'One of nature's miracles,' Harry said, smiling. 'The whole process is supplemented by a secondary form of hearing called bone conduction, in which sound waves set up vibrations in the skull bones that pass directly into the inner ear. This type of hearing affects the way you hear your own voice, for instance. That's why you sound different when you hear a recording of yourself speaking on an answer phone message.'

'So it's not just because I've been using my telephone voice, as my daughter calls it,' Elaine replied wryly.

Harry laughed. 'No. You're probably no more guilty of that crime than anyone else is. Anyway, the Rinne test—that's the name of the tuning-fork test—helps us to determine if hearing loss is sensorineural or conductive. In a normal ear, air conduction of sound waves is greater than bone conduction.'

'I see. It's really fascinating to know how your ears actually work but I suppose what I really want to know is if you think I have Ménière's disease?'

'While I can't rule it out at this stage, I can't say for certain that you are suffering from it either.' Harry turned to the computer and opened up the standard letter to request a hospital appointment. He filled in Elaine's details as he continued. 'It could turn out that you're suffering from inflammation of the middle ear, probably caused by an upper respiratory tract infection. If pus has been accumulating over a period of time, it could be the cause of the deafness and other symptoms you've been experiencing. I'll send a letter to the ENT clinic, requesting an appointment for you to go for a hearing test. The tests I've done are very basic and they will be able to perform far more stringent tests to diagnose the problem.'

'I hope so.' She sighed. 'It's the uncertainty that is worst of all. I know it's silly but I just want to know for definite if it is Ménière's.'

'Of course you do.'

He finished printing out the letter and placed it on the desk, wondering if this was an instance when he should do as Grace had suggested and phone the consultant. After all, the patient did appear to be extremely anxious, and with good cause, too.

'I'll give the hospital a call tomorrow instead of sending them a letter,' he said, making up his mind. 'It might help to speed things up a bit if I try a personal approach.'

'Oh, thank you, Doctor.' The woman smiled at him in relief. 'It would be awful if I had to wait months for an appointment before I find out the prognosis.'

'I'm sure the ENT consultant will fit you in just as soon as he can,' Harry assured her.

He saw her out then went back to his desk and picked up the letter. Normally he wouldn't have dreamt of going to such lengths, so what had made him change his mind today? Perhaps it was the fact that he knew it was what Grace would have wanted him to do.

He sighed as he screwed the letter into a ball and tossed it into the waste-paper basket. Grace had made it abundantly clear what she thought of him that afternoon. Trying to impress her would be a complete and utter waste of his time.

CHAPTER NINE

GRACE was exhausted by the time evening surgery ended and the day still wasn't over. She had promised Penny she would go to the hospital that night to visit Miles. She glanced at her watch as she opened the consulting-room door and sighed. There wasn't going to be much left of the evening by the time she got home again.

'Careful.'

She stopped dead and just managed to avoid running into Harry, who happened to be walking along the corridor at that moment. 'Sorry. I wasn't looking where I was going.'

'Too busy checking how long you have left before the coach turns back into a pumpkin?' he suggested with a teasing smile.

'I wish!'

Grace drummed up a laugh, hoping it would disguise how self-conscious she felt around him. She had been stunned when Harry had announced that afternoon that he was looking for commitment. The idea of Harry having a long-term relationship with a woman was impossible to imagine, even though he had sounded completely sincere. She knew he had expected her to say something at the time but she'd been too shocked. It was only after she'd had time to mull over the idea on the drive back to the surgery that she'd realised he would probably change his mind once he'd had a taste of monogamy—just like her own father had done. Men like Harry and her father were incapable of remaining faithful to one woman. They were genetically programmed to have multiple affairs.

'There's no chance of me going to the ball tonight,' she said quickly, wondering why her realisation hurt so much. She knew what Harry was like and it was silly to feel disappointed that he would revert to type. 'I promised Penny I'd visit Miles so that's my evening accounted for.'

'Mine, too.' He shrugged when she looked at him in surprise. 'When I phoned the hospital at lunchtime I just got the usual reply that Miles had had a comfortable night. I'd prefer to see for myself how he's doing.'

'Oh, but I'm sure Miles will understand if you don't have the time to visit him,' she protested rather too quickly, and he laughed.

'Now, now, Grace, you're not trying to put me off, are you?'

'I was just thinking of you,' she murmured without much conviction, because it was exactly what she'd been doing. 'It's been a busy day and you must be tired

'I'm touched.' He placed his hand on his heart and leered at her. 'You *do* care.'

'Oh, grow up, Harry.'

She stalked past him and made her way to the office to check that Janet had set the answering-machine before she'd left. They used an on-call service after surgery hours ended so any emergency calls needed to be redirected. Once she was sure the system was running she switched off the lights. Harry was lounging in the doorway when she turned round and she felt a little shiver run through her when she realised that he had been watching her.

'I'm sorry, Grace. I didn't mean to wind you up. I know

you must be tired, too, so how about we go to the hospital together? I'll drive so you can sit back and have a rest.'

'No, thank you. I'm quite capable of driving myself there.' She headed for the door then stopped when he made no attempt to get out of her way. 'Excuse me,' she said with icy politeness.

'Do I take it that the ceasefire has ended and normal hostilities have resumed?'

'You can take it any way you like,' she snapped. 'I am far too tired to play games with you, Harry. I just want to go to the hospital and see Miles, then go home to bed. Now, if you'll excuse me…'

This time he stepped aside to let her pass. Grace didn't look at him again as she hurried to her room to collect her coat and bag. By the time she got back, he'd left. She set the alarm then locked the doors and got into her car. It was usually a twenty-minute drive to the hospital, although it would take longer because of the snow, but she didn't care. She needed some time on her own to calm herself down.

She wasn't going to let Harry upset her, she certainly wasn't going to allow him to disrupt the even tenor of her life. She had made up her mind a long time ago that no man would exert that much influence over her. Maybe she was missing out in some respects, but at least she wouldn't have to suffer the heartache that followed a broken relationship. She'd seen how destructive love could be, had watched as her mother had changed from a confident, outgoing woman to someone who'd had no interest in life. Grace had sworn she would never allow the same thing to happen to her. Love might be wonderful while it lasted but it was hell when it ended. It was easier to remain single than risk getting hurt, even though at times she found herself wondering what it would be like to have someone special in her life.

Unbidden, a picture of Harry sprang to her mind but she quickly dismissed it. Harry was the last man she would want to share her life with.

Miles had been moved to a side room off the main ward. There was no sign of Penny when Harry arrived so he tapped on the door and went in.

'You don't look too bad, considering,' he said, as he deposited the bag of grapes he'd bought on the way onto the bed. 'Sure you're not malingering so you can get some time off work?'

'No way.' Miles retorted, looking affronted. 'I can think of better places to be than stuck in this bed if I was skiving off work, can't you?'

'Hmm, it's not my idea of a fun time,' Harry agreed, whipping Miles's chart out of its holder. He glanced through it and nodded. 'Looks as though everything is settling down now.'

'I hope so.' Miles grimaced. 'It scared the pants off me, I can tell you. I honestly thought my number was up last night.'

'And so it will be if you don't do something about the way you've been living recently.' Harry put the chart back and pulled up a chair. 'You've been pushing yourself far too hard and you have to stop. You won't help Penny or the baby if you make yourself ill.'

'I know. I knew I was doing too much but it's difficult to stop when so many people are depending on you.'

'I understand that, but you have to think about yourself for a change, Miles. You need to take time out, the same as everyone does.'

'It isn't that simple,' Miles protested. 'The practice has expanded in the last couple of years. There's a new housing estate been built on the edge of the town and a lot of the people from there have signed on with us.'

'So hire another doctor or take on a third partner. There's only so much that you and Grace can do in any given day.'

'We have talked about taking on another partner,' Miles admitted. 'The problem is finding someone suitable.'

'Someone who meets Grace's exacting standards, you mean?' He sighed when Miles didn't answer. 'I know you're far too loyal to admit that I'm right, but you have to make Grace see sense. You two need help and she really can't afford to be too choosy.'

'She isn't being deliberately difficult, Harry. It's not easy to find someone who's keen to work in the country. I mean, it's hard enough to find a decent locum, let alone somebody who wants to work here permanently.'

'I understand all that,' Harry assured him, realising this was the opening he needed to come clean about his report. 'I never got the chance to tell you last night but I'm working on a report for that new health service committee I'm on, about the problems rural GPs have to face. I've spoken to dozens of general practitioners in the last few weeks and they are all experiencing similar problems—too many patients and not enough staff to keep on top of the work.'

'At least we're not alone in this,' Miles said dryly. 'That's some comfort, I suppose.' He suddenly frowned. 'Have you told Grace about this report?'

'Not yet,' Harry admitted. He shrugged when Miles looked at him. 'I was waiting for the right moment. Knowing how Grace feels about me, she'll probably think I'm trying to undermine the work you do by finding fault.'

'Then don't tell her,' Miles said quickly. 'There's no point stirring things up when you two have to work together. You can tell her about the report after you've left Ferndale.'

'I don't know if I'd feel comfortable about that,' Harry said slowly. 'It doesn't seem right to leave her in the dark.'

'I appreciate how you feel, Harry, but it's not as though you planned on this happening. You had no idea that you'd end up working in the practice, did you?'

'Not initially—no. But after you told me about the problems you were having, I decided to volunteer my services.' He shrugged. 'I thought we could do each other a favour. I'd help you over a difficult patch and get some hands-on experience of the problems you're facing while I was at it. I was going to suggest it to you and Grace last night, in fact.'

'Only I threw a spanner in the works and ended up in here.'

'Something like that.'

'Well, I for one am more than happy with the idea.'

'Good. Now I just need to convince Grace.'

'And what if you can't and she refuses to co-operate? It would make it impossible for you two to carry on working together, and then what would happen to the practice? There is no way that Grace can manage on her own.'

Harry frowned when he saw how agitated Miles was becoming. 'I'm sure Grace realises that she needs help,' he said soothingly, but his friend refused to be mollified.

'I'm sure she does. But she could still refuse to work with *you* and that's the last thing I want to happen at the moment. Agh.'

Miles clutched his chest—he was obviously having chest pains again. Harry went to fetch the nurse, who quickly administered a spray of glyceryl trinitrate under his tongue. The drug was a powerful vasodilator, widening the blood vessels by relaxing the surrounding muscles. It had an immediate effect on Miles, much to Harry's relief. However, he knew that he couldn't risk upsetting Miles again. As soon as the nurse left, he set about reassuring him.

'I don't want you worrying, Miles. You need to concentrate on getting better. If you feel it would be best not to mention the report to Grace then I won't say anything to her at the moment. It's not as though I'm intending to base my findings solely on what happens at your practice,' he added, trying to square it with his conscience. 'As I told you, I've interviewed dozens of GPs and they've all told me much the same thing.'

'Thanks. I'd feel a lot happier if you didn't say anything to her right now,' Miles admitted, relaxing back against the pillows.

'Fine. I'll leave it for now. It's not a big deal.'

Harry tried to sound positive, although he wasn't happy about keeping a secret from Grace. She would be angry and upset when she found out and she would be justified to feel that way, too. Normally the thought of inciting her wrath didn't bother him; he quite enjoyed their spats, in fact. This was different, though. She had every right to be angry with him for withholding information and the thought troubled him.

'What's not a big deal? It sounds as though you two are plotting something.'

Harry glanced round as Penny came into the room. Grace was with her and he felt his stomach sink as he wondered how much of the conversation she'd heard. He offered Penny his chair, trying to ignore the look Grace gave him. She was obviously suspicious and he felt worse than ever. He wanted to tell her the truth but how could he when it might upset Miles again?

'We're not plotting anything, are we, Harry?' Miles denied.

'Of course not.' Harry avoided Grace's eyes as he edged

towards the door, deeming it wiser to make his escape before she could ask him any awkward questions. 'I'd better be off. I'll pop in again tomorrow night to see you.'

'He won't be here,' Penny announced. 'I've just had a word with the senior registrar and he said that Miles can go home tomorrow so long as he promises to rest. They're convinced that it was a stress-related angina attack.'

'That's wonderful news!' Harry exclaimed.

'Isn't it just,' Penny agreed happily. 'I can't tell you how grateful I am to you for stepping in while Miles recuperates. The registrar said that if he has the time to rest and avoids any undue stress for the next few weeks, he should be fine.'

'I'm sure Grace and I can handle things at the surgery,' Harry assured her, realising that there was no way he could risk causing another upset now. He would have to hide his report from Grace, even though he hated to think that he was deceiving her in any way.

The thought added to his growing sense of guilt. He quickly excused himself and left. However, as he made his way to the exit he could feel his deception weighing him down. Grace deserved to be told the truth, but how could he risk telling her when she might react the way Miles had predicted?

All of a sudden he found himself wishing that he done something to resolve the situation before now. Most relationships evolved over the years but he and Grace seemed to be stuck in a time warp. Was it his fault, was it hers, or were they both to blame? Were they both afraid of what might happen if they altered the parameters?

Harry stopped dead. He didn't want to admit that it might be the answer but he couldn't rule it out. He and Grace were afraid to stop fighting in case they ended up liking each other instead. Now that he had admitted the possibility, he realised that it explained so much. He'd never quarrelled with anyone the way he did with her, had never wanted to either. Hell, he didn't care enough to expend that much emotional energy. But it was different with Grace, very different. When he was with her he felt more fired up, more angry, more…everything! What on earth did it mean?

'Excuse me.'

Harry hastily moved aside when he realised that he was blocking the exit. He went back inside the building, knowing that he wasn't in a fit state to drive right then. The café was closed, but there was a drinks machine in the foyer so he fed some coins into the slot and was rewarded with a plastic cup of tepid coffee.

He took it over to a table and sat down, wondering how he was going to sort out this mess. It wouldn't be easy because he wasn't used to dealing with his emotions. Usually he kept them firmly battened down but they seemed to have been running riot recently— ever since he'd arrived in Ferndale, in fact, and seen Grace again.

He groaned. Everything kept coming back to Grace, didn't it?

Grace was crossing the foyer when she spotted Harry sitting at a table near the door. Although Miles had denied it, she couldn't shake off the feeling that there'd been something going on when she had arrived. There had been no chance to pursue it while Penny had been there, but if Miles and Harry were plotting something, she intended to find out what was going on.

She changed direction and headed over to the table. Harry seemed to be lost in thought and didn't notice her approaching. He jumped when she pulled out a chair and sat down.

'Grace.'

'What's going on, Harry? You and Miles are up to something, aren't you?'

'What makes you think that?' he countered, picking up the cup of coffee he'd bought.

'Intuition? A lucky guess?' she parried, not wanting him to suspect how anxious she was to get to the bottom of this mystery. 'You can call it what you like, Harry, but I want to know what is going on.'

'There's nothing going on. Miles was just worried in case I did anything to upset you. He was concerned about what would happen to the practice if we fell out.'

'And that's all it was?' she demanded, not sure if she believed him.

'Yes.' He shrugged. 'I told him everything was fine and I hope I managed to convince him. The last thing we want is for him to start fretting about work.'

'It certainly wouldn't help in his present state. I know Penny made it sound as though Miles is on the road to recovery, but the registrar stressed how important it is that he should avoid any pressure.'

'And worrying about you and me fighting isn't going to help.' Harry sighed. 'We can't go on like this, Grace. It's ridiculous for two intelligent people to be at each other's throats all the time. I really don't know why we've let the situation continue for so long, do you?'

'Habit?' she suggested flippantly, because there was something rather too intent about the way he was looking at her.

'And that's all it is—habit?' he said quietly, his eyes holding hers fast.

'Of course. Why, what else could it be?'

'I'm not sure. Maybe we argue because it's easier to stick with what we know than let our relationship develop.'

His eyes were very blue as he looked at her now and

Grace shivered. She wasn't sure exactly what he was implying but the comment alarmed her. As far as she was concerned, she and Harry had never had a relationship of any description and they never would.

'Or maybe we argue because we're not on the same wavelength,' she said, briskly discounting the suggestion.

'You really believe that? You think we're such opposites that we have nothing at all in common?'

'Yes, probably,' she said quickly, then wished she'd sounded more positive. After all, it was what she had always believed so why had she allowed an element of doubt to creep into her voice?

'What about the fact that we're both doctors? That's one thing we have in common. And we both care about Miles and Penny, so that's something else.'

'OK, yes. We do have some things in common. But you have to admit that we are poles apart in other respects,' she said defensively.

'I don't know how can you make such a judgement.' He leant across the table and she could see the urgency in his eyes. 'We have never sat down and had a proper discussion about anything in the whole time we've known each other, Grace. So how can you possibly claim that we have a completely different outlook on life?'

'I don't know. It's just how I feel.'

'Not very logical, though, is it?' he scoffed.

'Maybe it's not logical but I know all I need to know about men like you.'

'Men like me... What's that supposed to mean?'

'That you are exactly like my father,' She shot to her feet, wishing he would just accept what she was telling him and let it go. But, oh no, Harry always had to win the battle, although he wasn't going to win it this time.

'I learned from an early age what men like you and my

father are like, Harry. He too was charming, handsome, witty, but he had one major flaw. He was pathologically incapable of being faithful to my mother. And that's all the proof I need to know that you and I have nothing whatsoever in common.'

CHAPTER TEN

GRACE regretted her outburst as soon as the words were out of her mouth but it was too late by then. Harry rose to his feet and she could see the shock on his face. 'Grace, I—'

'No. I don't want to hear it, Harry.'

Spinning round on her heel, she ran towards the exit, uncaring that she was making a fool of herself. The only thing she cared about was putting some distance between herself and the man who had caused her to overreact as she had. She ran across the car park and got into her car, her hands trembling as she slotted the key into the ignition. She knew that Harry might follow her and the last thing she wanted was to talk to him after what had happened.

Tears welled to her eyes and she had to blink them away so she could see where she was going as she drove out of the car park. Fortunately, the roads had been gritted, which made driving a little less hazardous. Even so, she was relieved when she reached the turning for the village. Just another few miles and she would be home.

The thought had barely crossed her mind when the wheels hit a patch of ice and she screamed as the car suddenly spun out of control and careered across the road. There was a sickening crunch as the front bumper collided with a wall before the vehicle came to a juddering halt.

The air bag had deployed on impact so it took Grace a moment to free herself and open the door. She climbed out slowly, feeling sick and shaken as she realised how lucky she'd been. The front of the car had been crushed by the force of the collision, and if she'd been going any faster she wouldn't have stood a chance. She could have been killed, and the realization, combined with shock, made her cry, great hacking sobs that racked her whole body. She could have died out here on this lonely stretch of road and nobody would have known about it. Nobody would have cared.

'Grace. My God, are you all right? Here, sit down.'

All of a sudden Harry was there, his face looking pinched and white in the headlights. Grace didn't have the strength to argue as he helped her to his car and sat her down on the passenger seat. He crouched in front of her, his hands gentle as they probed her legs then her arms.

'I don't think you've broken anything.' He looked up and she could see the fear in his eyes. For some reason it made her feel a little better to know that he had been scared for her. At least somebody cared what happened to her.

'Does it hurt anywhere—your neck or your back— anywhere at all?'

'I don't think so.'

'Just let me check you over to make sure.'

He gently pushed her hands out of the way. Grace sat quite still as he felt his way around her neck and down her spine. Maybe she should have tried harder to convince him that she was fine, but it seemed to require too much effort.

'I can't find anything obviously wrong with you but you'll need to be X-rayed before I can be sure. I'll take you back to the hospital and—'

'No. I don't want to go back to the hospital, Harry. I just want to go home.' She sighed when he started to object. 'All right, I'm a bit shaken up, and I'll admit it. But otherwise I'm fine. Really, I am.'

He sat back on his haunches and looked at her. 'You wouldn't allow one of your patients to go home if they'd had an accident like this, would you?'

'Probably not.' She dredged up a smile. 'But the difference is that I know there's nothing wrong with me. I just need to go home and I'll be fighting fit again in the morning.'

'Hmm, I think that worries me more than anything else.' He gave her a teasing grin as he stood up. 'All right, I'll take you home on one condition.'

'And that is?'

'That I stay the night at your house.'

'Oh, but that really isn't necessary—' she began, but he didn't allow her to finish.

'It's either that or I'm taking you straight back to the hospital. You know as well as I do that something could develop in the next few hours, and I don't intend to take any chances. It's your choice, Grace, so make up your mind which it's to be.'

'I want to go home,' she said shortly, because there was no point arguing when he was in this mood. Once Harry dug in his heels, it was impossible to shift him.

She sighed as he closed the car door and went to fetch her bag. Harry had been right when he'd said that it was time they called a halt to their constant bickering. They needed to put the past behind them and move on. They should have done it years ago but it was which direction they would move in that worried her most of all. While she was fighting with Harry, she knew exactly where she stood, but once they stopped there would no restrictions.

She glanced at him as he got back into the car and felt

her heart lurch in sudden panic. Deep down she knew that once hostilities ceased it would be only too easy to let herself like him.

Harry was relieved when he saw the sign marking the boundary of the village up ahead. The past hour had been the worst of in his entire life. He felt physically sick when he thought what could have happened to Grace. She could have been killed tonight in that crash and it would have been his fault, too.

He should never have allowed her to drive off like that, never have upset her in the first place. He should have had more sense than to push her when he could see that she was so distressed. Maybe she had taken him by surprise by comparing him to her father, but that was no excuse. His actions tonight could have resulted in a tragedy, and he would never forgive himself for the way he had behaved.

He drove through the village in silence, wondering how he was going to make amends for what he'd done. He wouldn't blame Grace if she refused to forgive him, but he had to try to make his peace with her. He was still trying to work out the best way to proceed when he drew up in front of her house, but there really wasn't an easy way. The only thing he could do was apologise and make sure she knew that he meant it.

'Before we go any further, I want to say how sorry I am. I had no right to push you so hard earlier and I regret it more than I can say.'

'You're no more to blame than me,' she said quietly, turning to look at him.

'Maybe.' He shrugged, not wanting to compound his errors by arguing with her again, and she sighed.

'Harry, it's not your fault that I crashed the car. I shouldn't have gone driving off like that in the first place.'

'But you wouldn't have done so if I hadn't upset you.' He captured her hand, feeling his heart bump painfully when he realised how small and slender her fingers felt compared to his. Grace was so feisty that he tended to forget how petite she was, but all of a sudden he was incredibly aware of the physical differences between them.

'I want us to stop this constant bickering,' he said thickly, because his mind seemed to have captured the idea and was running riot with it.

'It's what I want, too. It's time we moved on, isn't it, Harry?'

'Yes, it is.' He gave her hand a quick squeeze then let it go. He couldn't trust himself to sit there holding her hand in case he did something really stupid. Grace may have agreed that it was time to end hostilities but it didn't mean she was prepared to go to the other extreme. Nothing she'd said or done had ever hinted at the fact that she might be attracted to him.

He hastily got out of the car. Entertaining such thoughts would only lead to another disaster and he had to stop it. He hurried round to the passenger side and helped her out, putting his arm around her to assist her up the path.

'Have you got your key?' he asked, trying to ignore the feel of her body as it nestled against him. Normally Grace wouldn't have allowed him within several yards of her, but they were so close now that he could feel the soft curve of her breast brushing against the wall of his chest, feel her hip and her thigh pressed against his. He gritted his teeth because there was no doubt that her nearness was having a potent effect on him.

'It should be in my bag.' She bent over to open her bag then gasped. 'Oh…'

'Grace.' Harry's grip tightened as he looked at her concern. 'What's the matter?'

'Just a pain in my shoulder…'

She bit her lip and he could tell that she was trying not to cry. Reaching out, he took her bag from her. 'Shall I find the key for you?'

'Please. It should be in the side pocket. It's got a fob on it—a silver frog.'

He quickly found the key and unlocked the front door. 'Mind the step,' he warned, helping her into the hall. He shut the door then looked around to get his bearings. It was the first time he'd been to her house so he had no idea of the layout.

'The sitting room's through there.' She pointed to a door at the far side of the hall and Harry nodded.

'Right, let's get you sitting down then I can take a proper look at your shoulder.'

'It was just a twinge,' she protested, as he helped her into the sitting room.

'It looked like more than a twinge to me,' he said firmly, easing the coat off her shoulders and sitting her down on the sofa. He packed a cushion behind her back then raised his brows. 'Where exactly does it hurt?'

'Just here,' she admitted, pointing to a spot midway along her right clavicle.

'Let me see.'

Crouching down in front of her, he unbuttoned her blouse before she had time to protest. There was an area of heavy bruising extending at an angle from her clavicle right down to the centre of her chest. Harry traced it with his eyes, trying not to let his gaze stray. This was a professional consultation and he'd be damned if he would give in to his baser urges.

'It's from the seat belt,' he said, glancing up. 'When you crashed, you must have been thrown forward in your seat, causing the seat belt to lock. That's what's made all these bruises.'

'So you don't think I've broken anything?'

'No. I know it must hurt but you'd be in a lot more pain if you'd broken your collar-bone.'

'Thank heavens for that.' She gave him a quick smile as she started to button the front of her blouse but he could see the colour in her cheeks and knew that she was embarrassed about him examining her.

He hurriedly stood up, not wanting to add to her discomfort if he could avoid it. 'What I suggest you do is have a warm bath to soak away the aches and pains. It's amazing how many muscles get pulled when you have an accident like that. You'll be stiff as a board in the morning if you don't do something about it tonight.'

'Good idea.' She pulled a rueful face. 'I certainly don't want to be staggering around the surgery tomorrow. It won't exactly inspire confidence, will it?'

'You'll have to wait and see if you're up to going in to work,' he warned her.

'I don't have much choice. I can hardly go off sick while Miles is off.' She struggled to her feet. 'I'll be fine by the morning—you'll see.'

It was on the tip of Harry's tongue to tell her it wasn't a foregone conclusion that she would feel better the following day before he thought better of it. Hadn't they just agreed that they would stop all the bickering? He bit back a sigh, wondering if they would be able to keep to their pact. Arguing with Grace had become a habit over the years and it would be difficult to break it.

'Let's hope so. How about I make us something to eat while you have that bath? I don't know about you but I'm starving.'

'That would be great, if you wouldn't mind.' She made her way to the door then paused. 'I'd better show you where everything is kept first, hadn't I?'

'I'm sure I can manage,' he said firmly. 'You go and have your bath. I'll just poke around in the cupboards until I find what I need, if that's all right with you.'

'Of course it is. Just help yourself.'

She headed along the hall, taking her time as she climbed up the steep stairs. Harry waited at the bottom until she had reached the top safely then went in search of the kitchen. It wasn't difficult to find because there were just the two rooms on the ground floor—the sitting room and a big kitchen-dining room which had been furnished in a country style with a huge old scrubbed pine table and rush-seated chairs in the centre of the room.

It was light years away from the ultra-modern steel and granite luxury of his own kitchen in the dockside apartment where he lived in London, but he had to admit that he preferred it. It was much more homely and inviting. He could just imagine the room filled with a family, the kids—a boy and a girl—sitting at the table, doing their homework, while he and Grace cooked dinner for them all...

He caught himself up short, shocked by the direction his thoughts were taking. Grace may have agreed that they should try to get along with one another, but she certainly hadn't agreed to play a permanent role in his life. They would be right back where they'd started if she found out what he'd been thinking, so he'd better put the idea out of his head.

He went to the fridge and opened the door. There was a pack of lamb chops on a shelf and vegetables in the tray at the bottom so he set to work on their supper. But no matter how hard he tried to forget about it, that cosy little image stayed with him: he and Grace working side by side, making dinner for their kids. The worst thing of all was knowing that there was no chance of it coming true.

* * *

Grace sighed as she stretched out, full length, in the bath and let the hot water lap over her aching body. Now that the initial shock was wearing off, she felt much better—better, in fact, than she'd felt for ages. She had never realised what a strain it had been, fighting with Harry all the time. She had expended an awful lot of energy over the years, making sure she was continually on her guard when she was around him. Now the situation had changed and they could stop arguing and become friends.

She frowned because the idea of being Harry's friend was hard to imagine. Could she really see herself phoning him up for a chat, joking with him, treating him exactly the same way she treated Miles?

She tried to picture this new relationship but she just couldn't see it. She simply couldn't picture Harry in a similar role to the one Miles had always played in her life. Harry was vastly different to Miles. *She* felt differently about him.

Closing her eyes, she tried to work out how she felt about Harry now that hostilities had officially ended. It wasn't an easy thing to do because she had never tried to make a balanced judgement about him before. She'd allowed her prejudices about her father to influence her and that had skewed her view of him. It might help if she tried a more analytical approach, she decided. Listed his good points first then his bad points and compared the two.

Grace held up her hand and started to tick the good points off on her fingers. Number one had to be the fact that he was a brilliant doctor. Number two that he had proved himself to be a loyal friend by giving up his free time to help Miles. Point number three must be the way he had treated her that night after the accident—kindly and considerately.

A smile curved her lips because this was easier than she'd feared it would be. She ticked off point number four—he was handsome—and giggled. Maybe it wouldn't be admissible in a court of law but it was a point in his favour, as was point number five: he was sexy. If she was going to do this properly, she had to consider all the pros as well as all the cons.

She held up her other hand because she'd run out of fingers by then. Number six—he was charming; number seven—he was good company; number eight—he didn't take himself too seriously. Number nine could be the fact that he was looking for a proper relationship nowadays instead of just having a good time. And number ten…?

Grace thought hard but she couldn't come up with anything else. Still, she'd managed to find nine things she liked about Harry and that in itself was truly remarkable, given how she'd felt about him in the past. Now it was time to balance the good points with the bad but for some reason it was far more difficult to come up with a list of negatives. All she could manage was the fact that Harry reminded her of her father, yet it seemed grossly unfair now to judge him by another man's actions.

Why had she clung onto that idea all these years? Why had she never tried to see Harry for who he was—a compassionate, skilful doctor, a loyal and true friend? The fault hadn't lain with Harry but with herself. She had clung to old prejudices because she'd been afraid to let them go. She'd been too scared to admit that she was attracted to him.

A tremor passed through her but Grace knew it was time she faced the truth. The thought of falling in love had always terrified her. She had done everything in her power to prevent it happening. She had acted in much the same way that Harry had done, although to a far lesser degree. However, at the back of her mind she had known that the one person who could slip past her defences was Harry.

That was why she had fought so hard to drive him away, why she had made herself find things to dislike about him.

Now everything had changed and she had to find another way to deal with Harry, one that would keep her just as safe. Their relationship may have altered dramatically but the old fears were every bit as strong. She still didn't intend to risk her heart for any man. Including Harry.

CHAPTER ELEVEN

HARRY had supper ready by the time he heard Grace coming down the stairs. He turned as she came into the kitchen, trying to control the leap his heart gave when he saw her. Her hair was damp from her bath, curling softly around her face in wispy little curls. She hadn't bothered getting dressed again and was wearing a towelling robe over a pair of pyjamas, which had a pattern of kittens printed on them. She looked so young and so vulnerable as she stood there in the doorway that he had to fight down the urge to rush over and take her in his arms. Even though they had agreed to end hostilities, he doubted if she would appreciate such a display of emotion.

'Supper's just about ready,' he said, turning back to the stove.

'It smells delicious,' she said quietly, coming into the room.

'Lamb chops, mashed potatoes and broccoli, plus some hopefully not-too-lumpy gravy.' He gave her a quick grin, deeming it safer to keep the mood as light as possible. 'Making gravy is a skill I have yet to acquire, I'm afraid.'

'Do you want me to make it?' She returned his smile, although he couldn't help but notice the way her eyes seemed to skitter away from his.

'Yes, please,' he said firmly, hoping to dispel her nervousness about him being there. The last thing he wanted was to make her feel uncomfortable so he played up his shortcomings for all he was worth. 'The last time I made gravy I had to slice it up. It was too thick to pour it out of the jug.'

'It sounds disgusting.' She laughed and he was pleased to hear that some of the strain had disappeared from her voice.

'Believe me, it was.' He handed her the spoon and moved away from the stove. 'Right, it's all yours. Shall I lay the table?'

'Please.'

She took over the task of making the gravy while he found china and cutlery in the various cupboards and drawers. He laid places for them both at the table then glanced round. 'All I'm short of now is napkins.'

'They're in the top left drawer over there.'

'Thanks.' Harry went over to the drawer and took out two old linen napkins heavily trimmed with lace. 'These are beautiful,' he said admiringly, as he placed them on the table. 'Are they a family heirloom?'

'No. I found them in a flea market when we were in Leeds, doing our postgrad training.' She looked up and smiled. 'I can never resist old linen. I have drawers full of stuff which I've collected over the years. It's an addiction of mine, I'm afraid.'

'You could be addicted to worse things.'

'So I keep telling myself every time I'm tempted to add to my collection,' she retorted drolly, and he laughed.

'Maybe there's a self-help group you could join,' he suggested, his tongue very firmly lodged in his cheek.

'Linen lovers anonymous, you mean?' She immediately latched onto his train of thought and Harry grinned.

'That's it exactly. I can just imagine you standing up in front of all the other addicts…'

'My name is Grace and I'm addicted to buying old table linen,' she said on cue.

He burst out laughing. 'You're too good at this! Come on—confess. You've been practising, haven't you?'

'Now, that would be telling.'

She gave him a broad smile and this time it was Harry who had to look away. As he went to fetch some glasses, he could feel his heart racing. It was the first time that Grace had smiled at him without holding back, and the effect it had had on him was truly amazing. He realised with a sudden rush that he wanted her to do it again, wanted her to smile at him like that all the time. When Grace smiled at him that way, he felt as though he could overcome any obstacles, achieve all his dreams. What was going on? Why did he feel this way? Was it just the relief of being able to behave naturally with her after all the years they had spent fighting?

He tried to tell himself that's all it was but in his heart he knew the answer was more complicated than that, so complicated that once he worked it out, his life would never be the same again. What he needed to decide first of all was if he was ready to take that next life-changing step.

'That was absolutely delicious.'

Grace sat back in her seat with a sigh of contentment. Now that supper was over she was feeling surprisingly relaxed. Having Harry in her home was a new experience, but once she had got over her initial nervousness she had started to enjoy the evening. He was very good company and had kept her entertained with a string of amusing anecdotes, without monopolising the conversation. He seemed as happy to listen as he was to talk, drawing her out so that she had overcome her natural reserve and had found herself chatting away. He had the gift of making a person feel special. And she definitely felt special tonight.

'How about a top-up?' Harry picked up the bottle of wine they'd opened, but she shook her head. While it had been a very pleasant evening, it would be foolish to get too carried away. Harry may be charming and sociable but she didn't want to run the risk of falling completely under his spell, did she?

'No, thanks. I'd better not have any more. I don't want to feel groggy in the morning when I go into work,' she explained, deeming it safer to get the conversation back onto more familiar territory.

'*If* you go into work,' he corrected, putting the bottle back without adding any more wine to his own glass.

Grace sighed because she could tell he wasn't happy about the idea. 'There's just no way that I can take any time off at the moment, Harry. It's far too busy at the surgery and it isn't fair to you.'

'Don't worry about me. I'll cope. It's more important that you're fit and well.' He leant forward and she could see the determination in his beautiful blue eyes. 'You had a hell of a shock tonight, Grace, so don't go pushing yourself too hard.'

'I'm not. I feel absolutely fine so there's no reason why I shouldn't go to work tomorrow.' She stood up, wanting to end the conversation before it turned into another squabble, and gasped when her ribs spasmed painfully as she tried to straighten up.

'And that's an example of you feeling fine?' His dark brows drew together as he studied her ashen face. 'You're in pain, Grace, and I don't need to be a doctor to know that. The only thing you should be planning on doing tomorrow is resting.'

'I'll be all right once I've had a good night's sleep,' she

murmured, hoping she wasn't being overly optimistic. Although the pain had eased while she'd been in the bath, there was no denying that she was starting to feel very stiff now. She bit her lip as she pushed the heavy wooden chair under the table because just moving it back into its place seemed to demand an awful lot of effort.

Harry shook his head as he stood up. 'I doubt a night's sleep is going to make much difference. My bet is that you'll probably feel an awful lot worse by the morning.'

'Cheer me up, why don't you,' she retorted, stepping around him to take her plate to the sink.

'I'm not trying to upset you.' He caught hold of her arm and brought her to a halt. 'I just don't want you running yourself into the ground like Miles has been doing.'

'Afraid you might end up stuck here longer than you'd planned?' she shot back.

'No. I just can't bear to watch you making yourself ill.' He ran his hand up her arm under the sleeve of her robe and she shivered when she felt his fingers skating so delicately over her skin. 'Promise me that if you don't feel well tomorrow, you'll stay home and rest.'

'I have a job to do so I can't possibly make a promise like that,' she countered. She didn't appreciate Harry telling her what to do. Maybe he was only thinking about her welfare but she was too used to being in charge of her own life to welcome his interference. She opened her mouth to tell him that but his hand had started moving again.

Grace's breath caught as his fingers began their descent. His hand had reached her elbow now, the pad of his thumb coming to rest in the crook of her arm. She could feel the faint beat of his pulse tapping against her skin, feel her own pulse quicken in response as a rush of awareness surged through her. It was as though she could actually feel his fingers leaving an imprint on her skin, like fingerprints on a glass. The thought that he was putting his mark on her was so erotic that she shuddered and he must have felt the spasm as it passed through her.

'You're shivering—are you cold?'

'I'm fine,' she said quickly, but her body betrayed her. She bit her lip as another shiver rippled through her.

'I can feel you shaking. It could be delayed shock from the accident.'

His hand swooped down to her wrist before she could do anything to stop it and she closed her eyes in despair. She knew that her pulse was racing and in a moment Harry would know it too.

'Your pulse is way too fast. Do you feel dizzy or sick?'

'No, I'm fine,' she repeated, wishing he would accept what she was saying and stop questioning her. However, it was too much to hope that Harry would take the easy option.

'Then why are you shivering and your pulse racing? I'm not stupid, Grace. I can see for myself that something isn't right.'

'I'm fine,' she repeated woodenly once more.

He turned her to face him and his eyes were very gentle as he looked at her. 'There's nothing to be embarrassed about, Grace. Most people would be suffering from shock if they'd been through a similar experience to yours.' He drew her into his arms and held her. 'There's no need to be scared, though, because I won't let anything happen to you—promise.'

Grace swallowed as she felt a sob well into her throat. If he'd been more pushy, more forceful, more like the old Harry, she might have been able to control her emotions, but this new tender side he was showing her was more than she could withstand. She had been scared tonight, scared and shocked and…and…

A sob escaped from her lips and she heard him murmur something as he drew her closer. He cupped the back of her head, his long fingers gently stroking her damp hair. 'It's all right, Grace. Everything will be fine,' he crooned, and she cried all the harder because it had been a long time since anyone had held her and comforted her.

When she'd been growing up, she'd been the one who had done the comforting. She had comforted her mother time and again after her father's numerous affairs. There had been no time to deal with the effect it had been having on her when her mother had needed her support, so Grace had learned to ignore her own feelings. Now it was as though all the pain and anguish she had bottled up had found an outlet and she cried as she had never cried before.

'Shh, it's all right, sweetheart. You're safe. I've got you.'

Harry brushed his lips against her temple as he rocked her gently to and fro. There was nothing sexual about the kiss—it was merely a way to offer comfort the best way he knew, and it worked. Grace clung to him, needing his support as her composure ebbed away. She felt like a frightened child again—terrified that she wouldn't be able to cope—but if she held onto Harry, she would get through this. Harry would do everything in his power to help her.

Afterwards, she wasn't sure if it had been that thought which had broken down the very last barrier. All she knew was that she needed more than that gentle kiss from him. She turned her face up towards him, seeing the pain in his eyes as their gazes meshed.

'I can't bear to see you cry like this,' he murmured, his mouth just a breath away from her own. 'Tell me what I can do to help you, Grace.'

'This.'

All it took was a tiny fraction of a second to close the

gap between them yet it felt like an eon had passed because she was so hungry for the comfort he could give her. Their lips met and she felt the shock that rippled through him, felt him try to draw back, and clung even harder. She needed this kiss, needed it to erase the past and give her back the future, and maybe her need communicated itself to him.

All of a sudden his arms tightened around her and she heard him groan as he deepened the kiss. There was no hesitation now as he plundered her mouth, no hint that he wanted to stop. In a strange way, it was as though Harry's need was as great as her own, although she couldn't imagine why that should be and didn't try. This wasn't the time to examine their motives, to start having doubts.

He raised his head and she shivered when she saw the hunger in his eyes. 'Tell me to stop if it's not what you want, Grace.'

'It is.' She placed her hand flat on his chest, felt his heart thunder beneath her palm, and smiled at him. 'I don't want you to stop, Harry. I want to feel as though someone cares about me.'

A shadow darkened his eyes but he didn't say anything as he bent and kissed her again, a long drugging kiss that had her clinging to him. When he lifted her into his arms and carried her along the hall she didn't protest, didn't say anything at all. She didn't want to talk, she only wanted to feel.

He carried her up the stairs to her bedroom and laid her on the bed then sat down beside her and kissed her again, butterfly-soft kisses which filled her with delight. She'd been kissed before and had even had a couple of brief relationships when she'd been younger but no man had ever treated her so tenderly. It was as though Harry was cherishing her, and the thought made all the cold spots in her heart fill with warmth. Even though Harry didn't love her, at least she would have had a taste of how it might feel to be loved.

He unfastened the belt on her robe and pushed it off her shoulders with the utmost care. Grace knew that he was afraid of hurting her, but the aches and pains in her body seemed much more bearable now that she had found the perfect distraction. He unbuttoned her pyjama top then paused, his handsome face looking unusually grave in the lamplight.

'Are you absolutely sure about this, Grace? It isn't too late to stop—'

'Hush.' She pressed her fingers against his mouth, stopping the words because they weren't necessary. She knew exactly what she was doing and didn't need to re-consider her actions. She needed this night, needed his passion so she could start to heal.

She looked deep into his eyes so there would be no mistake about what she was saying. 'I want us to make love, Harry. I know exactly what I'm doing and I promise you that I won't regret it in the morning.'

'So long as you're sure,' he said quietly, his eyes searching hers.

'I am.'

He didn't say anything else as he lifted her hand to his mouth and kissed her palm. He placed it on the cover beside her then carefully parted the edges of her top and kissed the hollow between her breasts. Grace shuddered when she felt the warmth of his lips grazing over her skin. His mouth skimmed over her body, pausing to drop kisses along the way, and it was only when he reached her shoulder that she realised he had been following the mark the seat belt had made.

He kissed her collar-bone then let his lips skim along her jaw before he found her mouth again. He kissed her slowly, deeply and with great tenderness, his hands gently caressing her stomach, her waist, the curve of her right breast. Grace could feel her tension building as his fingers edged ever closer to her nipple but at the very last second they moved away to start the whole process all over again. She was shivering by the time his hand arrived at her nipple again, and didn't think she could stand it if he didn't touch her this time, but he did.

She moaned when she felt him rub the tiny bud until it tightened, then cried out when his head swooped down and she felt his mouth close over her. Sharp little needles of pleasure darted through her as he suckled her and she put her hand on his head, her fingers twisting in his hair as she urged him to continue. What little she knew about love-making hadn't prepared her for this.

He lavished the same attention on her other breast then stood up and stripped off his shirt and tossed it onto the floor. He grinned wolfishly as he lay down beside her and took her into his arms. 'Now we're even, aren't we?'

Grace laughed, enjoying the fact that even in the throes of passion he could tease her. 'No tops, just bottoms?'

'Got it in one.' He rewarded her with a kiss then took hold of her hand and placed it on his chest. 'Your turn. I wouldn't want you to accuse me of being a chauvinist.'

'Heaven forbid,' she murmured distractedly, because she didn't feel like talking when there were far more inter-esting things to do, like exploring the hard ridges of muscle across his broad chest, or comparing the texture of his skin—deliciously rough where the dark hair grew in whorls over his pectoral muscles, silky smooth in other places. Then there were his nipples, flat penny-sized discs that puckered invitingly when she ran her fingers ever so lightly across them…

'That's about all I can stand for now.'

He took control again, his hands trembling as they slipped inside the waistband of her pyjama pants. Grace lay quite still as he eased them off her hips and down her thighs. It had been a long time since she'd made love and she couldn't pretend that she didn't feel a little embarrassed about her nakedness. Yet when she saw the expression on Harry's face as he looked at her, she knew there was no need.

'You're beautiful, Grace. Absolutely perfect.'

He kissed her softly on the mouth then stood up and stripped off the rest of his own clothes. He lay down beside her and took her in his arms again, holding her so close that she was left in no doubt about how much he wanted her. But even then, when his hunger must have been almost unbearable, he still sought her permission first.

'I want to make love to you, Grace. Can I?'

The simple sweetness of the request touched her more than any amount of flowery phrases could have done. Leaning forward, she kissed him on the mouth, letting her kiss answer his question. They made love with a passion that reduced her to tears again, but she didn't care that she was at her most vulnerable. She had nothing to hide any more. Not from Harry. *Never* from Harry. Her friend and now her lover.

CHAPTER TWELVE

HARRY was wide awake by the time wintry sunlight began to seep through the curtains. He'd barely slept, his mind too full of what had happened to allow him to rest. It was hard to believe that he and Grace had made love last night but the proof was in the fact that she was lying beside him.

Had it been the right thing to do? he wondered for the umpteenth time. Should he have given in to his desire and her pleas? Only time would tell and the thought did little to ease his conscience. Grace had been upset last night and he should never have taken advantage of her.

'Don't.'

He looked round when she spoke, feeling his heart fill with tenderness as he saw that she was awake. She looked so lovely as she lay there that he wanted nothing more than to gather her into his arms and kiss her until every doubt disappeared. However, he knew it would be only a temporary reprieve. It would need more than kisses to make this situation feel right.

'Don't what?'

'Don't blame yourself for last night. I knew what I was doing, Harry.'

'Did you?'

She sighed when she heard the doubt in his voice. 'Yes.

You didn't force me, Harry. It was my decision and I'm glad it happened.'

'Really?' he asked, as a little of the guilt started to melt away. He rolled over onto his side and smoothed a strand of caramel-brown hair behind her ear. 'So I didn't take advantage of you at a weak moment?'

'No more than I took advantage of you.' She smiled back at him, her dove-grey eyes filled with laughter, and he chuckled.

'Maybe it's you who should be feeling guilty instead of me.'

'I might, if I thought you regretted what we'd done.' She sobered suddenly. 'You don't, do you?'

'No. I don't regret a single second of last night. How could I when it was the most wonderful experience I've ever had?'

'It's kind of you to say that but it isn't necessary. I know you've been out with a lot of women and I'm sure they were much better in bed than I'll ever be.'

He sighed. 'I'm not being kind, Grace. I'm telling you the truth. I admit that I've dated a lot of women, although not as many as you might think. However, it's always been sex in the past—pure and simple.'

'So what was last night, then?'

'I don't know,' he admitted roughly. He was getting into dangerous waters now. If it hadn't simply been sex then it had to have been something more. But how much more? That was the question.

He cupped her cheek in his hand, unsure how to explain his feelings when he didn't understand them himself. 'It was more than sex, Grace. I really care about you and that's what made it so special.'

'Thank you.' She turned her head and pressed her lips to his palm. 'I care about you, too, Harry. I'm just glad that we've managed to sort things out at last and can be friends.'

'Me, too,' he agreed, although at the back of his mind he knew friendship wasn't the only thing he wanted from her.

He chased away the thought in the most effective way he knew—with a kiss. They were both breathless when it ended but he knew he should call a halt before the situation became too fraught. Last night Grace had needed comfort and he'd been there to provide it, but he mustn't make the mistake of thinking that she needed him in her life on a permanent basis.

He thrust back the quilt, refusing to let himself dwell on how unhappy that thought made him feel. 'I'll grab first go in the shower if you don't mind. I'll have to scoot off back to the hotel and get changed before surgery starts.'

'I'll make some coffee while you're doing that,' she offered, swinging her legs over the side of the bed. She went to stand up and groaned. 'Oh, I am so stiff this morning.'

'It's the knock-on effect from that accident.' He frowned when he saw her wince as she bent to pick up her robe. 'You really aren't in a fit state to go into work, Grace. Why don't you stay here and rest? I can cover this morning's appointments and do the home visits. With a bit of luck you might feel better by this evening.'

'No, I can't take time off. It isn't fair to you or the patients.' She slid her arms into the robe and belted it around her waist. 'I'll get the coffee started.'

Harry knew it was pointless trying to persuade her. However, as he headed to the bathroom he decided that he would have a quiet word with Janet when he got into work and ask her to direct the bulk of the patients to him. That way Grace wouldn't end up tiring herself out, although he would have felt happier if she'd stayed home and rested.

He sighed because if it was up to him, he would make

sure she permanently reduced her workload. It was about time someone looked after her and he would be more than happy to do it if she would let him. Taking care of Grace wouldn't be a chore but a pleasure, and it was a strange thought for a man like him who had never wanted the responsibility of looking after someone else. However, it was different with Grace. Very different. Making sure she was safe and happy was more important than anything else.

Grace phoned the local garage after Harry left and arranged for the breakdown truck to collect her car. She also arranged to hire another car while her own was being repaired and asked for it to be delivered to the surgery. Harry had offered to collect her on his way back so all she had to do was get herself ready.

She took a hot shower, hoping the warm water would loosen up her aching muscles. She towelled herself dry then went into her bedroom, pausing in the doorway as she caught sight of the rumpled bed. All of a sudden the memory of what had happened the night before came rushing back and she shuddered as a wave of longing rushed through her once more.

She'd known that Harry would be a skilled lover but it had been more than just technique that had made the experience so amazing. He had made love to her with real emotion and it was a shock to realise he was capable of that amount of feeling. It was an even bigger shock to remember how she had responded. Had it been the fact that she had needed comfort so desperately? Or had it been more than that? Was it possible that she was falling in love with him?

Grace gasped. She had no idea where that thought had sprung from, but the sooner she put it out of her head the better. She hurriedly got dressed and was ready by the time Harry arrived ten minutes later. He got out of the car and came to help her, holding the door as she slid rather inelegantly into the passenger seat.

'Still feeling stiff?' he asked, bending to help her with the seat belt.

'Just a little.' She winced as she twisted round to slot the buckle into its holder. Every muscle seemed to be aching now so that even the slightest movement caused her a lot of pain. Her discomfort obviously showed because he frowned.

'Are you sure you want to go through with this, I can manage for a couple of days without you—honestly, I can.'

'No, I'll be fine.' She dredged up a smile. 'I'll work the kinks out better if I'm doing something.'

'If you say so.'

He closed the door then got into the driver's seat. It was obvious he thought she was making a mistake, even though he didn't say so. Grace was glad. She didn't want to risk spoiling their new-found harmony by squabbling over something so trivial. Janet was walking up the drive when they arrived at the surgery and she stopped when she saw Harry helping her out of the car.

'What on earth has happened? You look awful, Grace.'

'I hit a patch of ice last night on my way back from visiting Miles and crashed into a wall,' Grace explained, gritting her teeth as she straightened up.

'But that's terrible!' Janet exclaimed. 'Did you go back to the hospital and get yourself checked over?'

'There was no need.' Grace dredged up a smile. 'Harry checked me over and he seemed to think I was all right.'

'Oh, so you two were together when it happened?' Janet said quickly.

'Not exactly. Harry came along shortly after the accident had happened and drove me home.'

She felt the colour rush to her cheeks and turned away.

There was no way that she wanted Janet to know that Harry had spent the night with her. She didn't regret it but neither did she want people speculating about what had gone on. Last night had been too precious, too special, to allow it to become a topic for idle gossip.

Her heart ricocheted around her chest as once again she found herself wondering why it had meant so much. She'd needed comfort, Harry had supplied it, that should have been the end of the matter. But the harder she tried to convince herself it had been no more than that, the more difficult it was to believe it.

The morning flew past. Harry barely had time to draw breath between patients. He'd had a word with Janet and she'd agreed to steer the bulk of the appointments in his direction. One patient rapidly succeeded another until it reached a point where he couldn't remember most of the cases he'd dealt with. He looked up as his next patient arrived, wondering how many more people were waiting to be seen. At this rate it would be time for evening surgery before he reached the end of his morning list.

'I'm Dr Shaw,' he explained, as a young man came into the room. He waved him towards a chair. 'It's Alistair Blake, isn't it?' he asked, checking the patient's details against the form Janet had prepared for him. Alistair Blake wasn't registered with the practice so he'd had to fill in a temporary resident's form before he could be seen.

Harry checked that the information was correct then smiled at him.

'What seems to be the problem?'

'I don't really know, Doc. I just know that I don't feel right,' the young man explained in a strong Australian accent.

'How so?' Harry prompted. 'Do you feel sick or dizzy? Or do you have a temperature perhaps?'

'I think I might have a temperature. I've definitely been feeling all hot and sweaty recently and it can't be the weather.' The young man cast a disparaging glance out of the window. Harry laughed.

'It seems highly unlikely. So when did it all start?'

'A couple of weeks ago, not long after I started work at the farm, in fact.' Alistair sighed. 'I haven't said anything to the boss in case he lays me off. I'm travelling around Europe, you see, earning my keep by doing whatever jobs I can find. I've done farm work before so I thought I'd give it a go when I saw the ad in the local paper. There's not much in the way of work round here at this time of the year and I was glad to get it. The trouble is I've felt real crook ever since I started there.'

'I see. Have you noticed any other symptoms, apart from the fever?' Harry asked, opening up a new patient's file. Although Alistair wasn't on their list, it was important to maintain a full history in case it was needed in the future.

'I've had a headache on and off for a couple of days now,' Alistair admitted. He frowned as he thought back over what had happened recently. 'I've had a few other aches and pains, too, although it could be this cold weather that's caused them, I guess.'

'And that's it? The more details you can give me, the easier it will be for me to find out what's wrong with you.'

'Yeah, I think so… Oh, yeah, I've felt a bit breathless at odd times. I almost forgot about that.'

'Well, that sounds like enough to be going on with. I'd like to examine you so if you could strip off your sweater I'll listen to your chest first.'

Harry took his stethoscope off the desk and listened to

the young man's chest. There were definite wheezing sounds when Alistair breathed in and out. 'Do you suffer from asthma?'

'Nah, fit as a flea I am. Never had a day's sickness in my life.'

Harry grinned. 'It's not often I hear a patient claiming they're fit and healthy.'

'I don't suppose you do.' Alistair grimaced. 'I'm really lucky and I know it, too, but I'm not making this up, Doc. I really do feel crook.'

'I'm sure you do,' Harry agreed, coiling up the stethoscope. 'Which is why I want to get to the bottom of this. What I'd like you to do for me now is a pulmonary function test. Your lungs sounded a bit crackly when I was listening to your chest so we'll use a peak flow meter to assess the speed at which the air can flow out of your lungs.'

'Whatever you say.'

Harry fetched the meter and explained what he wanted the patient to do. 'I want you to take a good deep breath then blow into this tube for as long and as hard as you can.'

'A bit like the breathalyser the cops use,' Alistair observed cheerfully. He took a deep breath, blew into the tube then handed it back to Harry. 'That's the best I can do, mate.'

'Fine.' Harry checked the reading. It was lower than he would have expected for someone of Alistair's age and general level of fitness. He finished his examination but he couldn't find anything wrong with the young man, apart from some minor breathing problems. He sat down again, determined to get to the root of the problem.

'You said that your symptoms started when you went to work at the farm. Which farm is it, by the way?'

'World's End Farm. It's a bloody good name for it, too. It feels as though you've reached the end of the world when you see the place.'

'Oh, and why's that?' Harry asked curiously.

'It's just the way the place is run. Don't get me wrong, Doc. Bill, the boss, is a good sort. And he loves those cows of his—knows them all by name, he does—but the place is the pits.'

'I see. So what exactly is your job?'

'I do whatever needs doing, basically. I start the day by mucking out the cowshed then I feed the animals and help with the milking.' He shrugged. 'It's hard work but not exactly rocket science.'

'Do you use any kind of chemicals?' Harry asked, wondering if they could be the cause of the problem.

'Nah. Bill doesn't agree with using all that stuff. He's into organic farming in a big way.'

'Then we can rule out some sort of chemical reaction.' Harry frowned. 'What about the feed you give the animals?'

'It's mainly hay, with the addition of some grain.'

'And is it in good condition?' he said quickly, wondering if this might be the lead he was looking for. 'It's stored somewhere dry?

'I wish.' Alistair rolled his eyes. 'It's kept in one of the barns, although I don't know why Bill bothers, really. Part of the roof has caved in and we're always having to shift stuff around to keep it out of the rain. Only last week we had to throw out a heap of stuff because it had gone mouldy.'

Harry nodded because it seemed he was on the right track after all. 'I don't suppose you wear a mask when you're handling the feed, do you?'

'Nah.'

The young man looked so horrified that Harry laughed. 'Well, I'm afraid you might have to wear one if you intend to carry on working there. It sounds to me as though you have farmer's lung, which is an allergic reaction to the dust and spores that are found in mouldy hay and some types of grain.'

'You mean that I've made myself ill by breathing in all that muck?'

'I think it's highly likely, given everything you've told me.'

'So what happens now? I mean, can you cure me?'

'Yes, and the treatment is very simple, too.' Harry smiled at him. 'You'll either have to wear a mask or stop handling mouldy feed. Maybe you can persuade your boss to repair the barn.'

'I'll give it a go, although I'm not holding out too much hope. It might be easier to find another job.'

'Well, good luck, whatever you decide to do.'

Harry saw him out, making a note to check with Janet if there was anything he needed to do to reclaim the cost of Alistair's appointment. As a non-UK resident, Alistair had to pay for any health care he received. He sighed as he buzzed in his next patient because he could have done without the extra paperwork today of all days. Still, it was worth it if it took the pressure off Grace. She needed someone to watch out for her, someone she could turn to in a time of crisis, and he could do both of those things and more. Putting Grace at the very heart of his life would be the most satisfying thing he had ever done.

CHAPTER THIRTEEN

GRACE was relieved that her morning list was so light. Despite her insistence to Harry that she was capable of working, it was a real effort to keep going. By the time her last patient left she was more than ready for a break.

She made her way to the office and handed Janet the files she'd used. 'Good job it wasn't too busy this morning. I don't know how I'd have coped if I'd had to deal with the usual mad rush.'

'That's what Harry thought,' Janet replied, popping the files into the tray. 'He's so considerate, isn't he?'

Grace frowned. 'Sorry, I'm not with you.'

'Harry asked me to send as many people as possible in to see him this morning. He was worried about you doing too much after your accident and I think it was really lovely of him, too. It just shows how much he cares about you. Maybe you two should think about getting back together.'

'Back together,' Grace repeated, still reeling from the shock of learning that Harry had been issuing instructions to her staff.

'Mmm. He told me that you two had had a bit of a fling. I thought then that he was hoping you would get back together, and this just proves it.' Janet gave her a misty-eyed smile. 'He must think an awful lot of you, Grace, if he's prepared to give up his time to work here.'

'But he's doing it for Miles,' she protested. She felt a rush of heat invade her and hurried on, needing to convince Janet that she had misunderstood. 'Harry's decision to work here has absolutely nothing to do with me, I assure you.'

'If you say so.'

Janet treated her to another of those knowing smiles, making it clear that she didn't believe her. Grace went back to her room, wondering what she should do. It was difficult to claim the moral high ground and assert that nothing was going on between her and Harry after last night.

She groaned as she realised how complicated the situation had become. It might be easier to let Janet think what she liked rather than cause a fuss. However, one issue which did need clearing up was the way Harry had assumed control. She might have slept with him but she didn't intend to let him use that as a means to usurp her authority.

Grace crossed the corridor. Harry's door was open and he looked up as she went in. She felt a frisson run through her when he smiled at her.

'Hi, how are you feeling? Still a bit stiff and aching?'

'I'm fine,' she said shortly, although it was hard to hold onto her anger when he looked at her that way. She cleared her throat, refusing to get sidetracked before she'd even started. 'Janet just told me what you did…'

'I know I shouldn't have gone behind your back, Grace, but I was worried about you.' His blue eyes filled with warmth. 'I know what you're like. Once you get an idea into your head, it's impossible to shift it, but you really and truly aren't up to doing too much today.'

'I'll admit that I found it hard going this morning,' she said stiffly. 'But that still doesn't excuse what you did.

How would you like it if I started issuing instructions to your staff?'

'I'd hate it because, like you, I'm a control freak.' He got up and came around the desk. 'We have a lot in common, don't we? We're both stubborn and pig-headed. And we both think we know better than everyone else does.' He brushed a wisp of hair off her cheek and his eyes were tender. 'I'm sorry if I overstepped the mark this morning but I couldn't bear to watch you making yourself ill. Will you forgive me?'

'I suppose so,' she said quickly, because she didn't want him to know how much his words had touched her. Was that all it had needed? she wondered in amazement. A simple apology and everything had been sorted out. If they had tried this approach years ago, they would never have wasted so much time arguing. But, there again, she hadn't wanted them to stop fighting, hadn't wanted to run the risk of growing to like him. She'd wanted to keep Harry at a distance, but it was different now. Now she wanted him as close as possible, wanted him with her every day and every night. In fact, she couldn't imagine what her life was going to be like when he went back to London.

The thought was too difficult to deal with right then. It was a relief when Janet tapped on the door to tell them she was going for her lunch. Grace sighed when she saw the coy look the receptionist gave them before she left.

'Janet seems to have got it into her head that we were an item at some point.'

Harry groaned. 'It was just a silly misunderstanding. I made a comment the other day about us having a bit of a history. I meant all the arguing we've done, but Janet took it the wrong way and thought I meant we'd been romantically involved.'

'She does tend to jump to conclusions,' Grace agreed, then frowned when he laughed. 'What's so funny about that?'

'Nothing. It's just that if you'd found out about it a couple of days ago you would have had my guts for garters.'

'I wasn't *that* unreasonable.'

'Oh, yes, you were. You never gave me an inch, Grace. You were on my case from the first moment we met.'

'It wasn't all one-sided. You gave as good as you got.'

'Yes, I did.' He sat down on the edge of the desk and looked at her. 'But it was mainly because I refused to let you win. I never really understood why we found it so hard to get along until you told me that I reminded you of your father.'

Grace knew that he was waiting for her to explain; she also knew that he deserved to hear the truth. She owed him that after the years they had spent at loggerheads because of it.

'My father was like you in a lot of ways, Harry. He was handsome, charming and great fun to be around.'

'Sounds very positive so far,' he put in gently.

She shrugged. 'I wish it was all good but it wasn't. The downside was that Dad used his charm and good looks to attract women. He had so many affairs over the years that I lost count. To be honest, I didn't care in the end what he did. I was more concerned about the effect his philandering was having on my mother. It broke her heart and her spirit,' she added, her voice catching.

'Hell, I had no idea…' He broke off, obviously guessing she hadn't wanted to him to know. 'It must have been awful for you, Grace.'

'It was. I loved my dad, yet I had to watch him destroying my mum's life. She was such a confident woman in the beginning, but she changed over the years and became very withdrawn. Sh-she died shortly before I went to med school and I've always believed that it was because she felt there was nothing left to live for.'

'Did your parents get divorced?'

'No. Mum refused to talk about it whenever I suggested it to her.' She shrugged when Harry looked at her in surprise. 'I thought it would be better for her if she and Dad separated, but Mum wouldn't hear of it. She kept hoping he would see the error of his ways, I suppose.'

'Do you ever see your father?''

'No. He moved to New Zealand and remarried. I think he felt guilty about what happened so he hasn't kept in touch.'

'It must have been a nightmare for you, Grace. Going through all that when you were just a teenager. It makes me almost glad that my parents were never around while I was growing up.'

'What do you mean?'

'Exactly what I said.' He shrugged. 'I had a nanny until I was old enough to be shunted off to boarding school. My mother loathed small children because they were so messy, and my father was too involved in making money to bother with me. I only became of interest to them once I grew up, but it was a bit late by then to play the doting parents. Suffice it to say that we aren't exactly close. We send each other Christmas and birthday cards, and that's about it.'

'How awful. No child deserves to be made to feel as though they aren't wanted. My childhood wasn't ideal but I always knew my parents loved me.'

'You were lucky in that respect. There are a lot of folk out there whose parents never really care about them.' He smiled, making an obvious effort to appear upbeat. 'Still, it wasn't all bad. It taught me to stand on my own two feet at an early age, and I'm grateful for that.'

It had also taught him to avoid making any lasting commitments, and it was a sobering thought. Grace gave him a small smile, wondering why it worried her so much. 'We're a real pair, aren't we?'

'We certainly are. Obviously, we have a lot more in common than we suspected.'

'I wonder if that was part of the problem. We recognised something of ourselves in each other.'

'Please.' Harry held up his hand. 'It's been a heck of a busy morning and I don't think my poor brain is up to an in-depth conversation like this. What I need most of all is something to eat.'

Grace chuckled. 'You only have yourself to blame. If you hadn't decided to take on the role of my protector, you wouldn't be so worn out.'

'I know, I know. Next time you have a fight with a brick wall, I shall leave you to soldier on on your own.' His smile told her that he was joking and she laughed. He grinned as well. 'How about I treat you to lunch at the pub by way of an apology for poking my nose in where it wasn't wanted?'

'Sounds good to me.'

She turned towards the door then paused when Harry said softly, 'I'm glad we've managed to sort things out between us, Grace.'

'Me, too.'

She smiled at him, thinking how handsome he looked. He'd taken off his jacket and the pale blue shirt he was wearing made the most of his dark good looks. However, it wasn't just his looks that appealed to her, but Harry himself. He was kind and considerate, clever and fun to be with. He was everything a woman could want all rolled into one gorgeous package. If he could overcome his reluctance to commit, he would be her ideal soul mate.

The thought accompanied her back to her room and stayed with her while she combed her hair and applied a little more make-up to her face. Normally, she didn't bother too much about her appearance when she was working, but she felt like making more of an effort. She finished applying a soft gloss to her lips then studied her reflection.

There was a definite glow about her which she had never seen before. It was as though talking about the past had lifted a weight off her shoulders and she felt happier than she'd done in ages. She had a future to look forward to now, although the big question was what role Harry would play in it. Would he remain as a friend or would be become more than that? It all depended on what she and Harry wanted.

Grace popped the top back onto the tube of lip gloss. In her heart she knew she wanted Harry to be more than a friend. The problem was that she had no idea how he felt.

There was no sign of Grace when Harry went through to Reception. He sat down on a chair while he waited for her, thinking back over what she had told him about her father. For all these years he'd assumed that she had disliked him as a person, but now he could see that it hadn't been him but what he had represented. He could understand why she had been so wary of him but he wasn't like her father at all. He would never make a commitment and break it. He would never break a woman's heart. If Grace entrusted him with her heart, he would love and cherish her until his dying day.

The force of his feelings stunned him. He'd gone from arguing with Grace to falling in love with her in the blink of an eye. And yet was that really true? Hadn't he had years to develop these feelings for her?

It was as though a light had been switched on and he could see the situation clearly. For the past ten years he had thought about her, wondered about her reaction to him, felt more than a little aggrieved that she was the one woman he could never seem to charm. If he hadn't cared about her then he would have dismissed her as nothing more than a nuisance, but he had never been able to write Grace off. His feelings for her had developed so gradually that he hadn't realised what had been happening, but there was no doubt in his mind about how he felt. He loved her and all he had to do now was win her round to his way of thinking.

'Sorry. I didn't mean to keep you waiting.'

Harry shot to his feet when Grace suddenly appeared. He could feel his heart thundering as he dredge up a smile. 'I was glad of a breather.'

'If you're expecting any sympathy, you'll have a long wait. It's your own fault for interfering.'

'You're a hard woman,' he declared, deeming it wiser not to pour out his heart at that moment. It had been a shock for him to realise how he felt and there was no way of guessing how Grace would react if he declared his love. It might be better if he worked on improving her opinion of him. He opened the door and bowed. 'Your carriage awaits, my lady.'

She rolled her eyes as she swept past him. 'We're only going to the Dog and Duck so we can walk.'

Harry grimaced as he followed her out of the door. Not quite the response he'd hoped for. He waited while she locked the door then offered her his arm. 'The path might be a bit slippery so you'd better hang onto me.'

Grace shot an assessing look at the path. 'Janet has gritted it so there shouldn't be a problem.'

Harry sighed as she set off down the drive. He wasn't used to women who spurned his advances. Normally they were only too happy to let him minister to them, but Grace was different. She was too independent, too used to dealing with situations her own way. He smiled to himself because that was one of the reasons he loved her, of course.

The Dog and Duck was packed when they arrived but the landlord found them a table in the snug. Harry ordered a glass of orange juice for himself and Grace asked for the same. 'What do you fancy?' he asked, glancing up from the menu.

'I think I'll have the steak pie.'

'Me, too. Do I have to go to the bar and order the food there?' he asked, when he realised that a couple of people standing by the bar were holding menus.

'Yes. It shouldn't take long. They're very efficient, even though it's always so busy in here.'

Harry joined the queue. He placed their order and paid before going back to the table. Grace was talking to a middle-aged woman seated at a table nearby. She looked up and smiled when Harry came back. 'This is Sally Arnold—Ben's wife from Hilltop Farm.'

'Pleased to meet you, Mrs Arnold.' He shook hands then sat down as Sally smiled warmly at him.

'I was just thanking Dr Kennedy for everything she did yesterday. It goes without saying that I'm equally grateful to you. Ian and Jill have told me how wonderful you both were. If it hadn't been for you two, I could have lost most of my family yesterday.'

'How are they?' Harry asked, as the woman paused to wipe away a tear.

'Not too bad, all things considered. Jill's coming home this afternoon but Ian and Ben will have to stay in for a bit longer.' She bit her lip. 'The doctors are worried about Ian's leg, and Ben's foot is a real mess.'

'But they will recover from their injuries,' Grace said quietly.

'Yes. And it's all thanks to you two.' Sally's voice caught. 'The consultant made no bones about the fact that it could have been a lot worse if you hadn't gone up to the farm when you did. I'm truly grateful to you both.'

'All in a day's work,' Harry said lightly. 'Mind you, if anyone deserves praise, it's young Steven. He was the real hero of the hour.'

'So I believe.'

Sally beamed with delight and he saw Grace give him an approving smile for successfully distracting her. After Sally had left, Grace leant across the table and squeezed his hand.

'Thanks for that. Sally dotes on her family and it's been a real ordeal for her. Saying that about Steven really cheered her up.'

'It was only the truth.' He turned his hand over and captured hers, feeling his heart fit in an extra beat when she didn't pull away. Maybe it didn't need charm to win her over after all. Maybe all it needed was honesty and a willingness to open up.

He smiled at her, making no attempt to hold back the emotions he could feel bubbling inside him. If she realised that he loved her, so what? He had nothing to lose because the only thing that mattered to him now was her.

'It's easier to be honest, isn't it, Grace? That way there are fewer misunderstandings. I know I was guilty of hiding my feelings in the past, but I've changed in the last few days and it's all down to you.'

'Me?'

'Yes.' He gripped her hand, hoping his courage wouldn't desert him. He had to tell her how he felt soon or he would burst. 'Grace, I—'

'Two steak pie and chips.'

Harry jerked his hand back when the landlord arrived with their order. By the time they had sorted out cutlery and condiments, the moment had passed. He stole a glance at Grace but her expression gave away very little about her feelings. Was she relieved that they'd been interrupted, perhaps?

He sighed as he recognised that he needed to think before he acted again. Grace needed time to get used to the idea that he wasn't like her father, and it would be a mistake to rush her. Of course, the real problem was that everything was out of sequence. They'd made love last night before he'd understood he was *in love* with her. They needed to start at the beginning again and take things slowly. It would be at least two weeks before Miles was fit enough to return to work, and he would use them to full advantage to court her.

He smiled to himself as he made a start on his lunch. The thought of winning Grace's heart was the only incentive he needed to be patient.

CHAPTER FOURTEEN

SEVERAL times during the following weeks Grace felt she should pinch herself to prove that she wasn't dreaming. Her relationship with Harry seemed to be going from strength to strength. He was the perfect partner at work—efficient, thorough, amiable with the staff and courteous towards the patients. However, it was outside work that the biggest changes occurred.

Although there was no repeat of the night they had slept together, they spent a lot of time enjoying each other's company, and she was amazed to discover how much they had in common. By the start of the third week of his sojourn at the surgery, she knew that she was in love with him, although she still wasn't sure how he felt about her. Did Harry see her simply as a friend, or did she mean more to him than that?

The uncertainty nagged away at her day and night, making it difficult to concentrate. She found herself drifting off into a world of her own at odd moments during the day, and it was worrying to know that she was so easily distracted. She decided she needed to reduce the amount of time she spent with him so when he asked her out to dinner on Monday night, she refused.

'Thanks, but I need a night in to catch up on some of the jobs that have accumulated.'

'Are you sure I can't persuade you?' He grinned at her, his eyes full of a teasing warmth that made her insides melt. 'I was going to suggest that we try that new restaurant in Dalverston, The Blossoms. I believe the food is excellent.'

'It's very kind of you, Harry, but I don't think I can manage it tonight.' Grace summoned a smile, hoping he couldn't tell how hard it was to refuse. 'Why don't you see if Miles and Penny fancy a night out? They might enjoy a change of scene after being stuck at home for the past couple of weeks.'

'Good idea. I'll give Penny a call now and see how they're fixed,' he agreed, heading for the door. He paused and glanced back. 'If you change your mind, though, just let me know.'

'I won't,' Grace said firmly, before temptation overruled common sense.

She sighed as he disappeared into his own room. She knew that she would spend the night thinking about what she was missing so why didn't she admit defeat and go with him? Miles would be returning to work next week, which meant that Harry would no longer be needed. Once he went back to London, she might not see him again for ages, so what was the point of denying herself the pleasure of his company? This might be the last opportunity they had to spend any time together.

The thought was so depressing that it was hard to put it out of her mind. It was another busy day and her morning list was full. Mr and Mrs Clarke had brought Bethany in to discuss her treatment. The tests had confirmed that the child had acute lymphoblastic leukaemia and her parents, naturally, were extremely worried. Grace sat them down, knowing it was her job to reassure them.

'I'm glad you've come in today. I've had a copy of Bethany's notes from the hospital and I see that she is due to start her treatment this week. It must be a tough time for you.'

'It is.' Brian Clarke could barely hide his distress. 'The thought of her having to go through all that at her age...' His eyes filled with tears as he looked at his daughter sitting on her mother's knee.

'It's a lot for any child to cope with, but it's the best chance Bethany has of beating this horrible illness,' Grace said quietly, her heart going out to the poor man.

'So you do think that she'll beat it, Dr Kennedy?' Sandra Clarke put in quickly. 'I know the consultant said that the odds were very good, but we weren't sure if he was just saying that.'

'He wasn't,' Grace said firmly. 'The survival rates for children with this type of leukaemia are excellent nowadays. New drugs mean that more and more children are going into remission.'

'So Bethany really does have a good chance of beating this?' Brian asked hopefully.

'Yes, she does.' Grace glanced at the letter that had arrived from the hospital. 'There's no sign of blast cells in Beth's cerebrospinal fluid, which is a good sign. She will be given anticancer drugs to destroy the leukaemic cells then transfusions of blood and platelets. She will also need antibiotics because the treatment will destroy her immune system, leaving her highly susceptible to infection.'

'They mentioned something about a bone-marrow transplant,' Sandra said, as Bethany climbed down from her knee and went to play with the toys. 'Brian and I have offered to be tested, but what happens if we're not suitable?'

'There is a worldwide register of people who are willing to donate bone marrow so if it turns out that neither of you is suitable, Bethany's details will be checked against that.'

'Really? So if there's someone with the right bone marrow—in Australia, for instance—they would be able to donate?' Brian exclaimed.

'That's right. More and more people are adding their names to the list. You will be asked if you want to go on it after you're tested.'

'Oh, there's no question about that, is there, Sandra? Even if we can't help our Beth, it would be good to know that we could possibly help someone else's child.'

'That would be wonderful.' Grace smiled, thinking how generous it was of him to think about other parents at such a difficult time. 'A bone-marrow transplant used to be suggested only if the patient had relapsed, but these days it's offered during the first period of remission. I expect that's what Bethany's consultant will do.'

'Yes, he explained that was what would happen.' Brian glanced at his wife. 'Is there anything else we wanted to know? I can't seem to remember what I'm supposed to be doing at the moment.'

'It's only to be expected,' Grace assured him, when Sandra shook her head. She stood up and shook hands. 'If there's anything at all that you're worried about, don't hesitate to phone the surgery.'

'Thank you. We really appreciate that,' Sandra said, picking her daughter up and giving her a cuddle. 'Will you thank the other doctor for us, too? If it wasn't for him, our Beth might not have been diagnosed so quickly.'

'Of course. I'll pass on your message to him.'

Grace saw them out, sending up a silent prayer that the treatment would be a success. She saw the rest of her patients then cleared up in readiness for the afternoon. There was a mother and baby clinic that day so she would be kept busy, but she loved her job and couldn't imagine working anywhere else.

She frowned because Harry was just as passionate about his job. She couldn't imagine him wanting to leave London, especially now that he was involved with this new health service advisory committee. It made her see how difficult it would be to maintain a relationship with him once he returned to the South. Maybe she'd been right to refuse his invitation tonight. When Harry went home, she didn't want to be left behind nursing a broken heart.

Harry phoned Penny and made arrangements for them to go out for dinner. He was in two minds whether he wanted to bother after Grace had turned him down but in the end he couldn't bear the thought of sitting on his own in the hotel. It was his turn to do the home visits that afternoon so once he had collected his list from Janet, he set off.

The snow had cleared now and the countryside looked green and fresh as he drove along the winding lanes. He had forgotten how beautiful it could be after living in the city for so long. How would he feel about working here on a permanent basis? he wondered as he stopped outside his first call. Once upon a time, the thought of leaving the city would have filled him with dread, but the more he thought about it, the more appealing it became. No crazy traffic, no fumes, no dirt, none of the hustle and bustle that marked his day. He could move here and set down roots, play a part in the local community, become a person instead of just another statistic. He would also be closer to Grace.

He sighed as he got out of the car because who was he kidding? It wasn't the thought of a beautiful environment, or any of the other benefits that were behind this sudden desire to relocate: it was Grace. He didn't want to leave her here and go back to London. He couldn't bear the thought of them living hundreds of miles apart. He wanted to see her every day, not just when it was convenient to fit a visit into their schedules.

It would mean a massive change for him but he was willing to make it if it meant they could be together. But was it what Grace wanted? She'd given no indication that she was interested in him in any way other than as a friend, and the thought added to his feelings of hopelessness. He couldn't go making plans for the future until he knew how she felt about him.

There were over a dozen mums booked into the clinic so Grace had her work cut out for her. Normally their practice nurse would have helped her, but Alison's ankle hadn't healed well enough yet for her to return to work so Grace was on her own. It was after four when she finished and evening surgery should have started.

'Here's your list.' Janet looked harassed as she handed her a list of patients. 'There's a couple of extras on there, I'm afraid, because Harry isn't back yet.'

'He's late.' Grace checked her watch. 'Has there been a problem at one of his calls?'

'I've no idea. He hasn't phoned in.' Janet grabbed the phone when it started ringing again. 'Ferndale Surgery. Janet speaking.'

Grace went back to her office and picked up the phone. Harry was meticulous about time-keeping and she couldn't help wondering what had happened to him. She dialled his mobile number but there was no reply. She left a message, asking him to get in touch with the surgery, and hung up. He might have been delayed by traffic, of course. The roads around the village were extremely busy at this time of the day with all the traffic from the local schools. He was probably sitting in a traffic jam at this very moment, in fact.

She buzzed Janet and asked her to let her know as soon as Harry arrived then called in her first patient. One appointment rapidly followed another but Janet didn't phone to tell her that he was back. By the time her last patient left, Grace was really starting to worry.

She hurried through to Reception. 'Still no news from Harry?'

'Not a peep.' Janet sounded concerned, too. 'It's not like him. If he's ever delayed, he makes a point of ringing in to let me know where he is.'

'Have you got a list of the calls he was supposed to do?' Grace asked. 'Maybe we can backtrack and find out where he's got to. For all we know, his car might have broken down and he's stuck in the middle of nowhere with no mobile phone signal.'

'Of course. Why didn't I think of that.' Janet hunted through the papers on her desk and pulled out a list of the day's house calls.

Grace took it from her and ripped it in two. 'We'll share it between us. That way we can contact everyone faster.'

She gave Janet one half of the list then took the other half to her room and began calling each of the numbers in turn. As soon as she was sure that Harry had been there, she ticked the address off the list. She worked her way down to the very last call of the day, a visit to Parson's Farm, and dialled the number, but the phone line was dead.

She went back to Reception. Janet had just finished calling the last number on her half of the list. She looked up when Grace appeared.

'Have you found him?'

'No. He turned up at every one of the calls I checked. How about you?'

'Same here. Do you think we should contact the police?'

Grace's heart sank, although she knew they would have to do so if he didn't turn up soon. 'Maybe we should wait another half-hour in case he's broken down.' She put her section of the list on the desk and pointed to the last call. 'I couldn't get through when I tried phoning this number. The line was dead.'

'Sorry, I should have mentioned that,' Janet apologised. 'The call didn't actually come from the farm. Apparently, they've got problems with their phone line and the message was passed on by someone else.'

'I see.' Grace went to the map pinned on the wall behind the desk. Parson's Farm was on the eastern boundary of their catchment area and she knew from experience that there was no mobile phone signal there.

'Did the caller give any details?' she asked, glancing at Janet. 'They're new tenants on that farm and I don't really know them. I've only seen them once when they came in to register.'

'The caller just said to tell the doctor that Mrs Norris was poorly and could the doctor come out to see her.' Janet looked guilty. 'It was really busy so I didn't get any more information out of him, I'm afraid.'

'Never mind.' Grace bit back a sigh. There was no point blaming Janet. 'Can you get Mrs Norris's file for me? I'll see if there's anything in it that might give me a clue.'

Janet found the file for her but there was very little information in it. Lucy Norris didn't appear to visit the doctor very often so there was no indication of why she would have requested a home visit. Grace came to a swift decision.

'I'm going to drive over there and see what's happened.'

'But Harry might not be there,' Janet protested.

'No, but I can't just sit here and wait for him to turn up. If he gets in contact in the meantime, call me, will you?'

'Of course.'

Janet looked troubled as Grace went to fetch her coat but there was nothing else she could think of that might help to solve the mystery of Harry's disappearance. She got into her car and her hands were trembling as she started the engine. She didn't think she could bear it if anything had happened to him. Harry meant the whole world to her and when she found him, she would tell him that and to hell with the consequences. She would rather take the risk of having her heart broken than live with the thought that she'd lost him because she'd been too scared to tell him how she felt.

CHAPTER FIFTEEN

HARRY was already running late by the time he arrived at Parson's Farm. Several of the calls he'd done that afternoon had taken longer than he'd expected. It was almost four o'clock by the time he drew up in front of the farmhouse so there was no hope of him getting back in time for evening surgery.

He took his mobile phone out of his pocket so he could ring Janet and groaned when he found that there was no signal up here. There were blank spots throughout this part of Cumbria and it was just his luck that he was in one now when he needed to make a call. He got out of the car and lifted his case out of the back then knocked on the farmhouse door. There was no reply so he knocked again and thought he heard someone shout this time. He tried the door and discovered it was open so he let himself in.

'Hello—it's Dr Shaw from Ferndale Surgery. Is anyone home?'

'I'm in here, Doctor,' a voice replied.

Harry followed the sound and found himself in the sitting room. There was a young woman lying on the settee and it was obvious that she was in a great deal of pain. He hurried across the room and crouched down beside her.

'Can you tell me what's happened?'

'It's the baby. I think it must be coming,' she whispered, pushing back the hand-knitted blanket that was covering her.

Harry's heart sank when he saw her distended abdomen. It was a long time since he'd delivered a baby and on that occasion it had been in the safety of a top London teaching hospital. It would be a vastly different experience, bringing a child into the world in this farm-house.

'When did you go into labour?'

'I had backache all last night and again this morning. I was shifting some bales of hay around the barn yesterday so I thought I'd pulled a muscle. I wasn't going to bother you but the feed rep called this morning and he insisted on phoning the surgery. Our phone's not working...some sort of problem with the line, apparently.'

'He was right to call,' Harry agreed, his hands moving gently over her swollen belly. 'How many weeks pregnant are you?'

'About thirty-five, or -six, I think.'

'You think?' His brows rose. 'Didn't the hospital give you an exact date when you went for your last check-up?'

'I haven't been to the hospital,' she admitted, then groaned as another contraction began.

Harry waited until it had passed before he questioned her further.

'Have you had any medical care at all? There was nothing in your file so it doesn't appear that you've been visiting the surgery for check-ups either.'

'There was no need. I mean, having a baby is a completely natural thing to do. Jed and I decided when we found out that I was pregnant that we were going to have this child with as little medical intervention as possible.'

'I see.' Harry was hard pressed to disguise his dismay

but it wouldn't achieve anything to tell her what he thought about such a crazy idea. 'I take it that Jed is your husband. Where is he now?'

'He had to go to Harrogate to visit his mother. She hasn't been well recently, you see. He won't be back until tomorrow night.'

She stopped as another contraction began. Harry waited until it had passed then checked to see if there was any sign of the baby's head crowning, not that he thought there would be. If he wasn't mistaken, the child was lying in the breech position, which meant that its bottom would be delivered first rather than its head. It was a situation that potentially could cause a lot of complications for both mother and child.

'Lucy, I think your baby might be lying the wrong way round,' he explained gently. 'From what I can tell, it's going to be a breech delivery.'

'Is that why it's so hard to push it out?' Lucy asked, her eyes glazing with pain.

Harry nodded. 'Yes. In a normal delivery, the birth canal stretches as the baby's head passes through it. That makes it easier for the rest of its body to follow. In your case, though, the baby's head will be delivered last and we need to make sure that he doesn't get stuck.'

Tears welled to the young woman's eyes. 'Would they have known my baby was breech if I'd gone to the hospital?'

'Yes, they would. They might have been able to turn it round, too, although some babies can turn themselves back again.' He patted her hand. 'The thing is, you didn't go to the hospital so we just have to do the best we can now.'

He stood up, wondering where the best place would be to deliver the baby. It struck him all of a sudden how cold it was in the room. There'd obviously been a fire in the grate but it had gone out, so his first task had to be to get it going again.

'I'll get the fire started again. We need to keep you warm and we'll definitely need to make sure your baby is warm when he or she arrives.'

'There's some logs outside the back door,' Lucy told him. 'There's also a basket of kindling there.'

'Right.'

Harry fetched the wood and set to work. Once he was sure the fire had caught, he put the guard around it then checked how Lucy was progressing. It was difficult to see what was happening, with her lying on the sofa, so he decided to make up a bed for her on the floor.

'I'm going to find some sheets and blankets,' he explained. 'It's a bit cramped on that sofa so I'm going to make you comfortable on the floor.'

'Do you think the baby will be all right?' she asked miserably.

'I don't see why not,' he said, trying to appear as upbeat as possible. There was no point adding to her distress by letting her see how worried he really was. So many things could go wrong during a breech presentation. If the baby's head was large, or the mother's pelvic girdle was unusually small, the child could get stuck. If Lucy had been seen at a hospital those points would have been taken into account and a Caesarean section arranged if it was deemed necessary. However, he didn't have that option so he would have to do the best he could.

He left her in the sitting room and ran upstairs to find some bedding, stripping the sheets and blankets off the bed in the main bedroom. Lucy was groaning when he went back to the sitting room—she was obviously in a great deal of pain. Harry dropped the bedding onto a chair and knelt beside her.

'I know it hurts, Lucy, but I can't give you any pain relief right now. It could affect your baby and that's the last thing we want.'

'I understand. I don't want to do anything that might harm it.' She bit her lip as another contraction began. 'It really does hurt.'

Harry held her hand until the pain had passed. He got up and quickly made up a bed for her on the floor in front of the fire.

'Here. Let me help you.' He put his arm around her and helped her to sit up. They had to wait while another contraction ran its course and he frowned as he realised that her contractions were coming really close together now. There wasn't even time for him to drive to an area where he could get phone reception because he didn't dare leave her.

He made her comfortable on the floor then checked the baby's position again. There was still no sign of it being born and he realised that he was going to have to do something to help it.

'I'm going to have to perform an episiotomy. Do you know what that is, Lucy?'

'I'm not sure,' she mumbled, her voice dulled with exhaustion.

'It's a small incision in the perineum—the tissue between the vagina and the anus. The perineal tissue hasn't stretched properly because your baby is coming bottom first. This will make it easier for him to be born.'

'I don't care what you do so long as he's all right,' she said weakly.

'Good girl.'

Harry stood up and hurried into the kitchen to wash his hands. He couldn't pretend that he wasn't becoming increasingly worried. Lucy was exhausted and had very little reserves of strength left to deliver her child. The sooner he got the baby out, the better.

He went back to the sitting room and put on some gloves then cleaned the area where he intended to make the incision. There was no time to worry about anaesthetic so he just did what had to be done. Lucy didn't seem aware of what was happening because she was in so much pain, but the procedure did seem to help. After a moment or two he could see the baby's buttocks descending.

'He's on his way. I'm going to try and help him along by pressing on the top of your uterus. It might be a bit uncomfortable but it's essential we get him out of there soon.'

He put one hand under the baby's bottom and applied gentle pressure to the top of the uterus and, inch by inch, the baby's body emerged. It was a little boy, although Harry barely had time to register the fact. They weren't over the worst yet because if the child's head got stuck in the pelvic girdle, he would be in real trouble. What he needed was another pair of hands to help him.

The thought had just crossed his mind when he heard a car draw up outside. There was a knock on the front door but there was no way that he could get up to answer it. 'Come in,' he shouted, praying that the caller would hear him.

They must have done because a moment later he heard footsteps in the hall and then the door opened and Grace appeared. Harry looked up at her and grinned.

'You have no idea how glad I am to see you!'

'You're doing great, Lucy. Now, when the next contraction starts I don't want you to push.' Grace squeezed the young woman's hand. 'We need to get his head out and we don't want to hurt him so we'll take things nice and slowly. It might help if you tried panting if the pain gets too bad.'

She looked up, feeling her heart jerk when she saw Harry was watching her. There was an expression on his face that made her feel all warm inside, but this wasn't the time to think about it. She nodded when she felt Lucy's hand grip hers as another contraction began. 'Here we go.'

Harry took firm hold of the tiny body, supporting it with his forearm as the baby's shoulders slid out. There was just the head now and that took a little longer. Grace was starting to wonder if it would ever happen when all of a sudden his chin emerged then the tip of an ear, followed by the rest of his head.

Harry cleared the child's nose and mouth of all the mucus then rubbed his back to encourage him to breathe. Grace could feel herself holding her own breath. It had been a difficult birth and so many things could have gone wrong…

The baby gave a gasping cry and Harry grinned. 'Well done, little fellow. I knew you could do it.' He passed him over to Grace. 'Can you clean some of the gunk off him while I cut the cord?'

'My pleasure.'

Grace smiled at him, knowing he could see a lot more in her expression than mere relief at such a happy outcome. He leant over and kissed her on the cheek, and his eyes were filled with tenderness.

'I'm glad you're here.'

He didn't say anything else but he didn't need to. Those few words were more than enough to tell her how he felt. Grace's heart felt as though it was going to explode with happiness as she gently dried the baby with a clean towel then wrapped him in a blanket. She placed him in his mother's arms.

'You have a beautiful baby boy, Lucy. Congratulations.'

'Is he all right?' Lucy peeled back the blanket so she could count his tiny fingers and toes.

Grace laughed. 'He's perfect. Have you decided what you're going to call him?'

'Gideon.' Lucy dropped a kiss on the baby's downy head. 'It's perfect for him, isn't it?'

'It is.' Grace smiled at her. 'A beautiful name for a beautiful baby boy.'

She let Lucy admire her son while she went to see if Harry needed any help. There was just the placenta to deliver now and it came away without any trouble. They cleared everything up then decided that Lucy would be more comfortable in a proper bed. One of them would have to go and phone for an ambulance, and it could take a while for it to get to the farm so there was no point leaving her lying on the floor.

Grace went upstairs and made the bed with fresh sheets and blankets then she carried baby Gideon upstairs while Harry carried Lucy. There was a lovely old wooden cradle beside the bed so she popped the infant into it and covered him up to make sure he was warm enough.

'Try and rest for a while, Lucy,' Harry advised the young mum. 'I'm going to phone for an ambulance to take you to the maternity unit. I know you said you didn't want any medical intervention but I think it would be silly to put yourself and Gideon at any further risk.'

'You're right.' Lucy flushed. 'It was a stupid thing to do. I should have gone to the hospital to be checked over.'

'You should. But there's no point worrying about that now.' Harry patted her hand then followed Grace out of the room. They made their way down the stairs and back into the sitting room. Harry sank down onto the sofa with a weary groan.

'I hope I never have to face a situation like that again.'

'Too much for you, was it?' Grace chuckled as she added another log to the fire.

'Way too much.' He looked up at her and smiled wryly. 'You must have nerves of steel if this is an example of the surprises that get thrown at you in the course of a working day.'

'The life of a rural GP is not as quiet as you might think, although, to be fair, I've usually had a bit of advance warning before I've been confronted with a situation like this.'

His eyebrows shot up into his hairline. 'You mean this wasn't a first for you?'

'Oh, no, I've delivered five babies since we opened the practice.'

Harry shook his head. 'As I said, you must have nerves of steel. Right, who's going to phone for the ambulance? Shall we toss a coin for it?'

'I'll do it. You sit here and get your breath back.' She smiled as she walked towards the door. 'You city types have more delicate sensibilities than us hardy rural folk.'

'Is that a fact?' He grabbed her hand as she passed him and hauled her down beside him. 'So you don't think I could cut it if I worked in the sticks?'

'Not a chance,' she scoffed, her heart beating like a mad thing because of the way he was looking at her. 'City living makes you soft—everyone knows that.'

'Do they indeed?' There was the faintest hint of threat in his deep voice and she shivered.

'Now who's the softie?' he taunted. 'You're not afraid, are you, Grace?'

'What's there to be afraid of?' she retorted, her eyes locked to his so that she saw the shimmer of heat that flared in them. 'There's nothing you can do that would scare me, Harry Shaw.'

'Really? So it doesn't worry you when I do this?' He ran his finger down her cheek then trailed it deliberately across her mouth.

'No,' she said, her voice sounding as though it was being put through a wringer.

'How about this?' He kissed her nose then her eyelids then the corner of her lips.

'I…um…'

He chuckled wickedly. 'Is that a yes or a no? You seem to be having difficulty making yourself understood. Maybe this will help.'

His head dipped and he kissed her on the mouth, a kiss that was filled with both tenderness and passion so that she was clinging to him by the time it ended. It was a second or two before she was able to gather her wits.

'I'd better sort out that ambulance,' she said hoarsely, standing up.

'Good idea.' Harry lay back against the cushion with a contented smile on his face. 'We can continue this discussion later, can't we?'

'If you want to,' she said, aiming for nonchalance and missing it by a mile.

'Oh, I want to all right. You can be absolutely sure about that.'

He gave her another of those breathtaking smiles but this time she didn't make the mistake of lingering. She hurried out to her car and drove down the lane until she reached a spot where she could receive a signal for her phone. She dialled the emergency services and requested an ambulance then let Janet know what was happening before she drove back to Parson's Farm—back to Harry.

She knew they had reached a milestone tonight but she was no longer afraid. A broken heart wasn't the worst thing that could happen to her—it was losing Harry. If there was a chance they could be together then there was no risk she wouldn't take to make it happen. Fear had stunted her life up till now but she refused to let it rob her of the future.

CHAPTER SIXTEEN

IT WAS gone seven by the time Lucy Norris was driven away to hospital in an ambulance. Harry locked the farmhouse door and slipped the key under a plant pot as Lucy had asked him to do. He turned to Grace, feeling his heart lift when he saw the happiness on her face. She looked so young and so beautiful that he couldn't resist kissing her.

'What was that for?' she asked, smiling up at him.

'Because you're beautiful.' He kissed her again then grinned. 'And because I enjoy kissing you.'

'Oh, I see. That explains it, then.' Reaching up, she kissed him this time. 'Ditto.'

Harry laughed as he put his arm around her shoulders and hugged her to his side. 'I don't think anyone's ever called me beautiful before.'

'That's their mistake. You are beautiful, Harry, inside and out. I just wish I'd realised it sooner.'

'Thank you.' He could barely speak for the lump in his throat. It was almost too much that Grace now thought of him as someone she could admire after the years they had spent trading insults. He led her over to the hire car and opened the door. 'I'll follow you back to the village. I need to write up my report so I'll head straight to the surgery.'

'You don't have to do it tonight. Leave it until the morning.'

'Are you sure?' he asked, not wanting her to think that he was shirking his job.

'Of course I'm sure. You've done more than your fair share tonight, Harry. You get off home and get ready for your night out.'

'Only if you'll come with me,' he said impulsively, taking her hand. 'I know you said that you had loads of things to do but won't you reconsider and come with me?'

'I'd love to come,' she said simply.

'Great.' He kissed her lightly on the mouth then dragged himself away before he got too carried away. 'I tell you what—why don't you follow me back to my hotel? I can get changed then we can call at your house on the way so you can get changed as well. I'll drive so you can leave your car at home.'

'That would be lovely,' she agreed, climbing behind the wheel.

Harry closed the door then strode over to his car. It didn't take them very long to get to his hotel. Grace parked in the car park and wound down her window when he came over to her.

'Why don't you wait inside while I'm getting ready? There's no point sitting out here in the cold.'

'If you're sure you don't mind,' she began, then laughed when he rolled his eyes. 'All right, I will.'

She followed him through Reception to the lift. His room was on the third floor and it only took a couple of minutes to reach it. Harry unlocked the door and switched on the lights.

'There's a mini-bar over there if you fancy a drink.' He pointed it out then headed for the bathroom. 'I'll just take a quick shower and be right back.'

Grace went over to the refrigerator and took out a bottle of fruit juice. She poured some into a glass then sat down to wait. She could hear the sound of running water coming from the bathroom, followed by the sound of Harry singing, and smiled to herself. He sounded so happy and carefree, and it was exactly how she felt, too.

He reappeared a short time later, wrapped in a thick towelling robe with his black hair glistening with water. 'I feel better after that.'

Grace put the glass on the table as her hand began to tremble. She knew she should say something but her mouth refused to obey the signals that were coming from her brain. He looked so gorgeously male as he stood there that she could barely think, let alone string any words together. The front of his robe was gaping open and she could see droplets caught in the dark hair that covered his chest. Her hands clenched because the desire to touch that warm, damp flesh was overwhelming.

Her eyes rose to his face and she saw the exact moment when he recognised what she was thinking. She was already rising to her feet when he strode across the room and hauled her into his arms. His mouth was hungry as it claimed hers but her response was every bit as greedy. She wanted this kiss—wanted Harry—just as much as he wanted her.

He picked her up and laid her on the bed then lay beside her, holding her so that she could feel his body pulsing with need. 'I want you, Grace,' he said, staring into her eyes.

'I know.' Lifting her hand, she smoothed the lines of tension between his brows. 'I want you, too, Harry. Just as much.'

He groaned as he bent and plundered her mouth again and she clung to him, needing to feel his strong arms around her. She had taken off her coat and he quickly dispensed with the rest of her clothing, his hands gentle and almost reverent as he traced the curve of her breast, the hollow of her waist, the flare of her hips. She knew that he was storing up the memory of how she looked tonight and her heart overflowed with happiness. This wasn't just some casual affair—it really meant something to him.

The thought unlocked the very last bit of her heart, the bit she had guarded so fiercely over the years. As she pulled him to her and kissed him hungrily, Grace knew there would be no turning back. She had given Harry her heart and her love, and he could do with them as he chose.

They made love with an urgency that left them both breathless. When Harry cradled her in his arms and pressed a gentle kiss on the top of her head, she could feel him trembling.

'Wow, that was amazing, wasn't it?'

'Mmm,' she replied dreamily, snuggling against him.

'Obviously a woman of few words,' he said, his voice tinged with laughter.

'You don't need me to tell you that you're a fantastic lover, Harry.'

'Actually, I do.' He drew back so that he could look into her eyes and she realised how serious he was. 'I don't care what anyone else has said in the past, Grace. Their opinion doesn't matter, but yours does.' He touched her cheek. 'I want to make you happy, darling.'

She was so touched that it was a moment before she could speak. 'You do make me happy, Harry. I can't remember ever feeling this happy in the whole of my life.'

'I'm glad.' He bent and kissed her then pulled her to him again. 'I've never felt this happy either.'

Grace sighed. Maybe he hadn't said he loved her in so many words but she knew it was what he had meant. Neither of them could have felt this way if they didn't love each other. They must have drifted off to sleep because the next thing she knew, the phone was ringing.

Harry groaned as he eased himself away from her and reached over to the bedside table. 'Harry Shaw… Miles! What time is it? Damn… No, you two go ahead and eat. We'll join you later. Yes, Grace has decided to come with us.'

Grace grinned as he replaced the receiver. 'I take it that was Miles, wanting to know where you'd got to.'

'It was.' He pulled her to him and kissed her. 'I forgot all about the time because I was too busy thinking about other things.'

'Very remiss of you, Dr Shaw.'

'It is, not that I'm solely to blame. You have a very distracting effect on me, Dr Kennedy.'

'Do I indeed?' She grinned up at him. 'What a pity that you told Miles we'd be joining them. I could have tested that theory.'

She didn't get the chance to finish before Harry whipped the phone off its rest. He punched in the number of the restaurant and asked to speak to Miles. Grace lay back on the pillow, stifling her laughter as he explained that something had cropped up and they wouldn't be able to make it after all. He hung up and smiled wolfishly at her.

'Now, what were you saying about testing out a theory?'

They spent the night sleeping in one another's arms. When Harry awoke the next morning, he knew he would treasure the memory of this night for the rest of his life. There wasn't a doubt in his mind that he wanted to spend all the rest of his nights and his days with Grace, too. He loved her and he believed that she felt the same way about him. However, before he asked her to share his life, he wanted to make sure she knew he was serious about making such a commitment. It would be a big step for both of them and he didn't want anything to go wrong, so he would wait until he had put everything in place before he declared himself.

As soon as he returned to London, he would hand in his notice and set about finding himself a job closer to Ferndale. There were a number of excellent hospitals in the region and it would be good to take on a fresh challenge, although if anyone had suggested it a few weeks ago, he would have laughed. However, he'd discovered that there were more important things than a glittering career and the accolades that came with it. There was Grace: she was all he needed.

It was hard to keep his plan a secret from her but Harry was determined to prove to her just how committed he was. He didn't say a word to her that day or the one that followed. Fortunately, they were so busy at work there wasn't time to talk about anything very much, and when it came to the nights, well, they had other things on their minds. By the end of the week, he knew he had found what had been missing all his life. He had found Grace, his soul mate.

Friday arrived and Miles called into the surgery to see them. He looked a lot better and was obviously keen to return to work. It was agreed that he would start the following Monday, which meant that Harry would no longer be needed. Miles and Penny invited him and Grace to dinner at their house on Saturday night as a small thank you for what he'd done, but Harry politely declined. He wanted to spend his last evening in Ferndale with Grace and nobody else.

They decided to eat in the hotel so he booked a table for them in the dining room. There was a function on that evening so the place was packed. Harry was in the lobby, waiting for Grace to arrive, when he spotted a GP he'd interviewed a few weeks earlier for his health service report. The man had been scathing about the benefits of the committee's work so it had been a frosty encounter. He nodded curtly when he saw Harry but didn't stop to speak to him.

Harry was grateful for that. Grace had arrived and he

was very much aware that he still hadn't told her about the report. Although he was sure she would understand, he didn't want anything to spoil their last evening together.

'You look gorgeous,' he said as he went to meet her. His eyes moved hungrily over the curves so beautifully displayed by the soft rose chiffon dress and she laughed.

'Naughty, naughty,' she admonished, wagging her finger at him. 'I am not on the menu.'

He captured her hand and placed a kiss in the centre of her palm. 'Not yet you aren't.'

He led her straight into the dining room, not wanting to waste time by having a drink in the bar because he could think of better ways to spend the evening. Grace sat down and looked around.

'It's busy in here tonight. Is there some kind of a function on?'

'So I believe.' Harry glanced up when the waiter appeared with the menus, trying to curb his impatience as the man described the various dishes on offer in lengthy detail.

Grace sighed when the waiter finally retreated. 'I thought he would never go, didn't you?'

'Yes.' Harry leant across the table and captured her hand. 'I'm not really interested in food at the moment.'

'Neither am I.' She placed her menu on the table and stood up. 'Why don't we order room service later?'

Harry followed her out of the dining room, pausing *en route* to tell the waiter that they had changed their minds. A generous tip soon quietened the man's protests and they were free to leave. He put his hand under Grace's arm as they walked to the lift, thinking about what was going to happen. Would he be able to hold back and not declare how he felt when he loved her so much?

'I see you've found yourself another stooge.'

Harry stopped as the GP he'd interviewed a few weeks

earlier came out of the bar and stood right in their path. The man had obviously had a couple of drinks because he was unsteady on his feet. Harry smiled politely, although his heart had sunk. The fellow was obviously out to make trouble.

'Good evening, Dr Grant. Are you here for a function?'

'The local rotary club's annual dinner,' the older man informed him, slurring his words. He turned to Grace. 'I hope you haven't been taken in by all that caring, sharing rubbish, Dr Kennedy?'

'I'm afraid I don't know what you're talking about.' Grace looked at Harry but before he could try to limit the damage by explaining, the older man cut in.

'This new health service advisory committee, of course. Dr Shaw has been doing the rounds of all the surgeries, asking questions and poking his nose in where it's not wanted. He claims that he wants to help us solve our problems, but I think that's highly unlikely, don't you?' He jabbed Harry in the chest. 'I know all about your reputation, Shaw. You don't give a damn about people like us. It's the glory you're after.'

He pushed past them without another word. Harry watched him walk towards the dining room, wondering if he should call him back and make him retract that statement. He did care—that was the only reason he had agreed to be on the blasted committee.

'Is it true?'

Grace's voice cut through the silence and his heart contracted when he heard the pain it held. He turned to her, seeing how pale she looked.

'No, of course not.'

'So you haven't been talking to other GPs in the area?'

'Yes, I have. But that doesn't have any bearing on what's happened between us, Grace.'

'Doesn't it? So why did you turn up in Ferndale in the first place?'

'OK, I'll admit that I wanted to talk to you and Miles so I could get some information for my report. I'll also admit that, initially, I wanted to work at the practice so I could experience the problems at first hand. But everything has changed since then, Grace. You know it has.'

'Do I?'

'Yes.' He captured her hands and held them tightly, praying he would be able to convince her that he was telling the truth. 'We've changed, too, haven't we?'

'I thought we had.'

Her voice was so cold that Harry shuddered. It felt as though they had gone right back to the way they'd been when he'd arrived in Ferndale, and it was all his fault. He should never have allowed Miles to persuade him not to tell her about the report, never should have kept it a secret from her. He should have told her the truth from the beginning but if he tried to explain it to her now, she would think he was passing the blame onto Miles.

'We've come a long way in the last couple of weeks, Grace,' he said urgently. 'Don't let a stupid misunderstanding spoil what we have.'

'I won't.' She withdrew her hands from his and there was something so final about the gesture that he could feel fear clutching his heart. 'It's the fact that you deliberately lied to me, Harry, that I can't forgive. Now, if you'll excuse me, I'd like to go home.'

'Grace, wait,' he cried, but she ignored him.

He ran after her but got held up near the door by a crowd of people who had just arrived. By the time he reached the forecourt, she was driving out of the gates. Every instinct was telling him to go after her, but what could he say if he did? He could tell her the truth, that he loved her, but he wasn't sure she would believe him after what had happened. He had lost her trust and it was going to be an almost impossible task to win it back. The thought that he might not succeed filled him with dread but he had to try. He would do what he'd planned to do—go back to London, hand in his notice and find another job in the area. Maybe, just maybe, it would convince Grace that he was serious.

Grace spent the weekend locked away in her house. She didn't even answer the phone in case it was Harry calling her. She didn't want to speak to him, certainly didn't want to hear any more of his lies. He had used her to further his own career and there was no point glossing over the truth with a lot of fine words. Oh, she didn't doubt that he had enjoyed making love to her, but it hadn't really meant anything to him. The fact that he hadn't made any plans to see her after he went back to London proved that.

What a fool she'd been to fall in love with him. She had thought he cared about her, but there was only one person Harry cared about and that was himself. Well, she hoped that his fact-finding mission had been a huge success. Then he wouldn't need to come back and she wouldn't have to see him ever again.

She felt grey and listless when she went into work on Monday morning. Miles was already there, looking remarkably chipper for a man who had been dicing with death. They ran through what had happened while he'd been away then made a start on morning surgery, and as the week progressed, it was as though Harry had never been there. It was only the empty ache in her heart that kept reminding her of his visit. Harry may have left but he was constantly on her mind.

* * *

Harry handed in his resignation as soon as he returned to London. According to the terms of his contract, he had to give three months' notice but the management team reluctantly agreed to take into account the fact that he had another month's leave owing to him. He would leave at the end of March and he could hardly wait. The sooner he was back in Cumbria, the sooner he could prove to Grace that he was serious about wanting to be with her. When he saw an advertisement for the post of Clinical Director at Dalverston General Hospital, it seemed heaven sent. He went for an interview and was delighted when he was offered the job. Maybe it was sign that his luck was changing.

It was a beautiful spring day when he drove back to Cumbria. He had rented out his London apartment and intended to stay at the hotel until he found a place to live. So much depended on what happened between him and Grace that there was no point even thinking about purchasing a property just yet. He went straight to the hotel and dumped his bags then drove to the surgery, wondering what kind of a reception he would receive. He hadn't even told Miles about his plans in case he told Grace, so it would be a shock for everyone when he turned up.

He drew up in the car park and got out of his car, and when he turned round there was Grace. Harry felt a huge wave of love envelop him as he looked at her. These past weeks had been a nightmare and he had missed her dreadfully. He wanted to rush over and take her in his arms, tell her that he loved her and had come back to claim her, but would she listen to him? And, most important of all, would she believe him?

CHAPTER SEVENTEEN

GRACE could feel the ground rushing up to meet her. For one terrible moment she thought she was going to faint. It was only when Harry started walking towards her that she managed to pull herself together.

She stood up straighter and glared at him. 'After for some more information for your report, Harry?'

'No. I came to see you.'

He stopped in front of her and she had to physically restrain herself from touching him by putting her hands behind her back. She had missed him so much that she had wondered if she would be able to carry on. She had missed hearing his voice, seeing him smile, feeling his touch— the list was endless. She had lain awake, night after night, remembering how it had been when he'd held her in his arms and made love to her.

'Don't. I can't bear to see you looking so unhappy, Grace.'

He reached out to stroke her cheek but she jerked her head away. 'Stop it. I don't know why you've come here today, Harry, but I'm not interested in anything you have to say. Is that clear?'

'Yes. I understand why you feel like that. But you have to let me explain—'

'Oh, no, I don't.' She laughed scornfully. 'That's where you are wrong. I don't have to listen to you or see you if I don't wish to do so.'

She brushed past him, shaking off his hand when he tried to detain her. She got into her car, forcing herself not to look at him as she drove out of the car park. She'd made a fool of herself over him once and she didn't intend to repeat her mistake. Harry could stand there all day and all night and she still wasn't going to listen to him.

He was still there when she got back from the house calls, sitting in his car and watching her. He hadn't moved when she left after evening surgery finished, but she ignored him. Miles was obviously delighted to see him but she got into her car and drove home without saying a word to him. She'd said everything she intended to say to Harry and there was nothing to add. He had used her and she, like a fool, had let him do it. What could either of them say to make this situation any better?

Harry felt as though he would go mad if Grace didn't listen to him soon. As the week progressed, she continued to ignore him, no matter what he did. He tried parking outside her house in the hope that she might relent if they were away from work, but it didn't happen. She came and went, and never even looked his way.

He tried leaving a message with Janet, asking Grace to phone him, but to no avail. There was no call that day or the next. Grace was determined that she wasn't going to have anything more to do with him and—short of kidnapping her—there was nothing he could do.

By the time he started work at Dalverston General he had given up any hope of getting through to her. He threw himself into his new job in the hope it would help to blot out the pain. There was certainly enough work to keep him busy during the day, but at night, when he went back to the hotel, he couldn't stop thinking about what he had lost. He had come so close to having everything a man could dream of, only to lose it again through his own stupidity.

Grace was putting in long hours at the surgery. Although Miles maintained that he was perfectly capable of doing his job, she insisted on taking over the extra tasks, like budgets and staffing issues. With Penny doing well and nearing the end of her second trimester, he didn't really need to start spending more time in the office. She finally managed to find them another locum so that took some of the pressure off, but even then she didn't let up. While she was working, she had less time to think about Harry and the mistakes she had made.

She heard on the grapevine that he was working in the area and although it surprised her to learn he had moved out of London, she refused to read anything into it. After all, Dalverston General was an excellent hospital and the post of Clinical Director was hardly a step down. Harry had seen the job as a good career move and the thought made her feel worse than ever. Not only had he managed to find sufficient information for his report while he'd been working at the surgery, he'd also secured himself a promotion.

It was the beginning of May when everything came to a head. Grace was in her office when Miles poked his head round the door.

Have you seen this?' he asked, holding up the latest issue of one of the medical journals they subscribed to.

'Not yet. Why, is there something interesting in it?' she asked, her attention more focused on what she was doing.

'It's Harry's report.' Miles placed the magazine on her

desk. 'It isn't the whole of it, naturally—it probably runs to hundreds of pages. But he's raised some bloody good points from what I've read. He really did get to grips with the issues we face.'

'Then it was worth his while working here,' she said tightly.

'It was.' Miles sighed. 'I feel really bad about swearing him to secrecy, Grace. It was a rotten thing to do.'

'What do you mean?'

'I made Harry promise not to tell you about this report. You two were always at each other's throats and I was terrified that you would take offence if you found out about it.' He smiled guiltily. 'Sorry. I should have had more faith in your professional judgement.'

'You made Harry promise not to tell me?' she said in bemusement. 'But how? When?'

'When he came to see me in hospital the night after I'd had the first angina attack. Oh, I could tell he wasn't happy about leaving you in the dark, but I thought it was the best thing to do in the circumstances.'

'You thought I would refuse to allow Harry to work here if I found out about the report?' she said, needing to get the facts clear in her own mind.

'Yes. I knew you wouldn't be able to cope on your own, so it seemed safer not to rock the boat.' Miles grimaced. 'I suppose I should have mentioned it before but I never thought about it after Harry left. Sorry.'

He gave her a quick smile and left. Grace picked up the journal and read the article. It only touched on the main issues that had been raised in the report but, as Miles had said, Harry had done an excellent job. Nobody reading the report would be in any doubt about the problems rural GPs faced.

Grace closed the magazine, feeling sick as she realised how badly she had misjudged Harry. He had been genuinely committed to making a difference to people's lives, as this report made clear. However, it was the fact that he had honoured his promise to Miles and not told her about it that caused her the most pain. She had judged his actions without knowing the true facts. She had allowed the old fears to surface, instead of listening to her heart, and she would never forgive herself for that.

She stood up. All she could do now was to try and make things right between them, although she wasn't foolish enough to think that he would forgive her. Why should he accept her apology when she had refused to listen when he had tried to explain?

Harry was in his office when his secretary phoned to say he had a visitor who insisted on seeing him. 'Ask them to make an appointment,' he said briskly. 'I have a finance meeting this afternoon and I need time to prepare for it.'

He hung up and reached for the file of papers then looked round in surprise when the door burst open. He stared at Grace, wondering if he was hallucinating...

'I'm sorry, Harry, but I need to speak to you now, not in a couple of weeks' time.'

Harry rose to his feet, shaking his head when his secretary tried to intervene. 'I'll deal with this, thank you.'

Grace closed the door and walked over to his desk. 'Miles just told me that he made you promise not to tell me about the report you were writing,' she said without any preamble.

'Did he?' He cleared his throat when he heard how hoarse he sounded. Grace's sudden appearance had knocked him for six, but he had to pull himself together. 'Is that why you've come here?'

'Of course.' She turned on her heel and marched back to the door then stood there, with her hand resting on the handle. 'I owe you an apology. I'm sorry for what I said that night. It was unfair of me to blame you.'

She went to open the door but Harry knew he couldn't let her leave. If she walked out of this room he might not get another chance to tell her how much he loved her. Just for a second his head swirled as the enormity of what he was doing hit him, before he grasped his courage in both hands.

'I love you, Grace.'

He heard her gasp and when she turned he could see the shock on her face.

'What did you say?'

'I said that I love you.' He crossed the room in a couple of strides and took hold of her hands. 'I love you,' he repeated, more gently this time. 'I wanted to tell you how I felt before I left Ferndale but I decided it would be better if I had everything in place before I did so.'

'In place?'

'I wanted to prove to you that I was capable of making such a huge commitment.' He squeezed her hands. 'That's why I resigned from my last job and accepted the position here. It would have put too much of a strain on us if we'd had to commute between here and London. I didn't want to take that risk.'

'You gave up your job *for me*?'

'For us,' he corrected her. 'Our relationship means more to me than anything else. You mean more to me than I can tell you.'

'I don't know what to say. I thought you'd used me...' Tears suddenly rolled down her cheeks and he gathered her into his arms and held her close.

'Please, don't cry, darling. I can't bear it.' He brushed her mouth with a gentle kiss. 'I love you so much and it's been agony, thinking that you hated me.'

'I don't hate you, Harry. I never did.' She cupped his

cheek in her hand, her eyes gazing at him with a wealth of love in them. 'I love you, too. I think I've always been more than a little in love with you, and that's why I fought so hard to keep you at a distance for all that time.'

'Do you mean it?' he demanded, his heart pounding. 'You're not just saying that because you know it's what I want to hear?'

She laughed softly. 'When have I ever tried to humour you?'

He grinned. 'Not very often.' He drew her to him and kissed her with a passion that soon had them clinging to one another. Pulling back, he groaned in dismay. 'Would you believe that I have a finance meeting in exactly twenty minutes' time?'

'Hmm, in that case, I'd better make myself scarce.' She zipped out of his arms and opened the door.

'Wait. You can't just leave like this. We need to talk and—'

'Definitely *and,*' she murmured wickedly. She waggled her fingers at him. 'I'll see you later. How about dinner at my house? That way I can guarantee there won't be any interruptions.'

'There had better not be.' Harry chuckled as he pulled her back into the room. He kissed her soundly, held her close so she could feel what her nearness was doing to him, then opened the door again.

Grace looked more than a little flushed when she left, much to his secretary's amusement. Harry didn't care. It didn't matter a scrap what anyone thought so long as Grace loved him.

That thought made him float through the rest of the day. Before he knew it, it was time to leave. He drove straight to Grace's house and parked outside, waiting for her to come home. As soon as he saw her car coming along the road, he got out. She opened the car door and stepped into his arms, and it was a homecoming in every sense of the word. He knew then that he was the luckiest man who had ever walked this earth. He had the woman he loved and he had the future to look forward to, a future they would share. Bending, he kissed her on the lips.

'I love you, Grace. I want to spend the rest of my life with you so will you marry me?'

'Yes.'

'You really mean it?' he exclaimed in amazement.

'Yes. Oh, I suppose I could pretend to be reluctant and make you wait for my answer, but what's the point when it's what we both want?' She took hold of his hand and led him to the door. 'We've wasted enough time in the last ten years, Harry, and I don't intend to waste another second, so why don't we go inside and celebrate?'

'A woman after my own heart,' he said, laughing as she dragged him into the house.

Reaching up on tiptoe, Grace wound her arms around his neck. 'That's all I want from you, Harry. Your heart.'

'It's yours. For ever,' he murmured, then stopped talking because he was far too busy kissing her.

Flowers make great gifts...until they wilt.
Chocolates are always popular...calories are not.
Baby daughters are just adorable...but they grow up!

Carly and Cici have both tried Plan A – being perfect wives and mothers. Now they're about to start over...with their darling daughters.

This collection of brand-new stories is the perfect gift for Mum – or yourself!

Available 2nd February 2007

Available at WHSmith, Tesco, ASDA, and all good bookshops

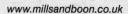

www.millsandboon.co.uk

M&B

4 FREE

BOOKS AND A SURPRISE GIFT!

We would like to take this opportunity to thank you for reading this Mills & Boon® book by offering you the chance to take FOUR more specially selected titles from the Medical Romance™ series absolutely FREE! We're also making this offer to introduce you to the benefits of the Mills & Boon® Reader Service™—

- ★ **FREE home delivery**
- ★ **FREE gifts and competitions**
- ★ **FREE monthly Newsletter**
- ★ **Exclusive Reader Service offers**
- ★ **Books available before they're in the shops**

Accepting these FREE books and gift places you under no obligation to buy, you may cancel at any time, even after receiving your free shipment. Simply complete your details below and return the entire page to the address below. You don't even need a stamp!

YES! Please send me 4 free Medical Romance books and a surprise gift. I understand that unless you hear from me. I will receive 6 superb new titles every month for just £2.80 each, postage and packing free. I am under no obligation to purchase any books and may cancel my subscription at any time. The free books and gift will be mine to keep in any case.

M7ZED

Ms/Mrs/Miss/Mr .... Initials ....
BLOCK CAPITALS PLEASE

Surname ....

Address ....

....

.... Postcode ....

Send this whole page to:
UK: FREEPOST CN81, Croydon, CR9 3WZ